She was even more beautiful than he remembered.

And just as cool and remote as she had been in California. But she was here now. At last he had Miss Josie McCall right where he wanted her. In *his* land, *his* domain.

It was only a matter of time. In the end his patience would be rewarded. It always had been. And Josie McCall was no different from any other woman. More of a challenge, perhaps, but he liked a challenge. It made the final result all the more enjoyable.

Prince Kumar leaned back in the limousine and smiled. She was a delectable woman, and he had every intention of sampling all that delectability.

Sooner or later.

He closed his eyes and felt his body grow hard with need. Shifting to try to ease his discomfort, he decided it would have to be sooner, rather than later....

Dear Reader,

The weather's hot, and here at Intimate Moments, so is the reading. Our leadoff title this month is a surefire winner: Judith Duncan's *That Same Old Feeling*. It's the second of her Wide Open Spaces trilogy, featuring the McCall family of Western Canada. It's also an American Hero title. After all, Canada is part of North America—and you'll be glad of that, once you fall in love with Chase McCall!

Our Romantic Traditions miniseries continues with *Desert Man*, by Barbara Faith, an Intimate Moments-style take on the ever-popular sheikh story line. And the rest of the month features irresistible reading from Alexandra Sellers, Kim Cates (with a sequel to *Uncertain Angels*, her first book for the line) and two new authors: Anita Meyer and Lauren Shelley.

In months to come, look for more fabulous reading from authors like Marilyn Pappano (starting a new miniseries called Southern Knights), Dallas Schulze and Kathleen Eagle—to name only a few. Whatever you do, don't miss these and all the Intimate Moments titles coming your way throughout the year.

Yours,

Leslie J. Wainger
Senior Editor and Editorial Coordinator

Please address questions and book requests to:
Silhouette Reader Service
U.S.: 3010 Walden Ave., P.O. Box 1325, Buffalo, NY 14269
Canadian: P.O. Box 609, Fort Erie, Ont. L2A 5X3

DESERT MAN

Barbara Faith

Silhouette® INTIMATE MOMENTS®

Published by Silhouette Books

America's Publisher of Contemporary Romance

SILHOUETTE BOOKS

ISBN 0-373-07578-2

DESERT MAN

Copyright © 1994 by Barbara Faith

All rights reserved. Except for use in any review, the reproduction
or utilization of this work in whole or in part in any form by any
electronic, mechanical or other means, now known or hereafter
invented, including xerography, photocopying and recording, or in
any information storage or retrieval system, is forbidden without
the written permission of the editorial office, Silhouette Books,
300 East 42nd Street, New York, NY 10017 U.S.A.

All characters in this book have no existence outside the imagination of
the author and have no relation whatsoever to anyone bearing the same
name or names. They are not even distantly inspired by any individual
known or unknown to the author, and all incidents are pure invention.

This edition published by arrangement with Harlequin Enterprises B. V.

® and TM are trademarks of Harlequin Enterprises B. V., used under
license. Trademarks indicated with ® are registered in the United States
Patent and Trademark Office, the Canadian Trade Marks Office and in
other countries.

Printed in U.S.A.

Books by Barbara Faith

BARBARA FAITH

is a true romantic who believes that love is a rare and precious gift. She has an endless fascination with the attraction a man and a woman from different cultures and backgrounds have for each other. She considers herself a good example of such an attraction, because she has been happily married for over twenty years to an ex-matador she met when she lived in Mexico.

Chapter 1

Two flights arrived at the Los Angeles International Airport at the same time that early autumn afternoon. One came from Paris via New York, the other from Guatemala by way of Mexico City. As both flights deplaned, over five hundred passengers hurried into the terminal and headed for Immigration. The line was long, the air inside September warm.

When the woman ahead of Josie McCall moved forward, Josie picked up her carryon valise, shifted the shoulder bag, gripped the suit bag and advanced two steps. She wished she'd sent everything through instead of carrying what she considered essential, not-to-be-lost items. But the wedding was the day after tomorrow and she'd been afraid to take a chance on losing either Jenny's wedding present or her own maid-of-honor dress.

For a moment she forgot the discomfort of having to stand in line and thought instead about the coming wedding. She had been both surprised and overjoyed when Jenny telephoned two weeks earlier to tell her that she was marrying Mike Brennan, the commando-type former Green Beret she'd hired to find the son her Arabian husband had taken from her.

The thought of Jenny's ex-husband, Aiden Hurani, sent a chill down Josie's back, and she was glad that after those terrible years of marriage to that damned Arab Jenny was finally finding happiness. With an American, thank God.

Maybe she was prejudiced, but darn it all she was happy as a clam that Jenny was marrying someone of her own kind.

The line moved forward. Josie started to pick up her bag but before she could a man in the line next to her said, "Please, let me help you."

He was tall, well dressed in an obviously expensive dark gray suit, and so good-looking she wondered with a touch of amusement why she hadn't noticed him before.

"Please," he said again. "It is difficult to manage so many things, yes?"

He had an accent. Italian? she wondered.

When she murmured a thank-you, he picked up the carryon bag and took the suit bag from her. "It's difficult when two international flights arrive at the same time," he said. "Were you on the New York flight, too?"

Josie shook her head. "No, I came from Guatemala."

"Guatemala?" He looked interested. "I have heard it is a beautiful country."

"It is." Josie inched forward, looked at her watch and frowned. "I have friends meeting me and I hate to keep them waiting."

"I, too, have friends who are expecting me. But there is nothing we can do, is there?" He smiled as though to reassure her. "What is the time here? I flew last night from Paris and I'm still on Paris time."

Josie checked her watch again. "Four-fifteen," she said. And thought, Paris? He doesn't sound French.

As they chatted she found herself wishing he would ask for a number where she could be reached. She was only going to be in California for a few days, but still...

The line moved ahead and when at last she saw there were only three people in front of her she took her passport out of her purse, and when the couple ahead of her moved toward the immigration officer she said, "Thank you for helping me," and reached for her bags.

He hesitated, as if reluctant to give them to her, and she thought for a moment he was going to ask for a phone number. But all he said was, "I hope you have a pleasant stay in Los Angeles."

"You, too." Josie offered her hand. "Thanks again. I appreciate your help."

She turned away and he watched her give the official her passport. The immigration officer studied it, handed it back and gave her an appreciative look when she moved off.

She was something to look at all right, the other man agreed. A tall, slender redhead, elegant in a smart black suit with a skirt that came three inches above her knees and high heels that showed off absolutely spectacular legs. When she started through the door that led to Customs he had a sudden urge to call out, "Wait a minute! What's your name? Do you have a number where I can call you?" But there was no time. The immigration fellow motioned him forward. He offered his passport, it was stamped, and he, too, moved on to collect his luggage.

He kept looking for her while he did, searching through the press of people while two carousels spilled out luggage and hordes of passengers jostled for a closer position. Just as the luggage from his flight started down the ramp he spotted her. But again, before he could call out she disappeared through the swinging doors that led to the outside waiting room. He swore under his breath and had a sudden and unreasonable feeling that someone very special had just slipped through his fingers.

"Josie!" The small blond woman broke away from the crowd and hurried forward. "I'm so glad to see you! Was your flight all right?" A quick hug, then a laugh bubbled and Jenny Cooper Hurani, soon to be Mrs. Mike Brennan, held her friend away from her and said, "You look so...so big-city beautiful. I guess because you've been living in Guatemala I expected you to arrive in jeans."

"That's what I wear most of the time, but today was special. I didn't want to look like a country cousin when I met the groom-to-be." Josie hugged her friend again and over her shoulder looked at the large man standing behind her. "Hi," she said. "You must be Mike."

He was tall, broad shouldered and rugged. He took her hand and said, "Glad to finally meet you. It was damned nice of you to come all this way for the wedding."

"I wouldn't have missed it, but I'm sorry I kept you waiting. My flight out of Mexico City was delayed." She picked up her carryon. "I'm all set, we can go now."

"Not yet," Jenny said. "We're waiting for Kumar."

"Kumar?"

"Kumar Ben Ari." Mike reached for her luggage. "Best man and best friend. His plane just got in, too."

"I thought I told you about him," Jenny said. "He has a business in Jahan and when Aiden took Timmie there, Mike called him. Kumar helped us get Timmie out of the country."

"He's from Jahan?" Josie lifted a questioning eyebrow. "Like Aiden?"

Mike shook his head. "No, Kumar's from Abdu Resaba. He has the title of both Prince and Sheikh, but he rarely uses either one."

"A desert sheikh." Josie's eyebrow raised another fraction of an inch when she looked at Jenny. "I thought you'd had your fill of Middle Eastern types."

Mike stiffened, but before he could say anything he spotted Kumar. "Hey!" he called out. "Over here!" and Josie turned to see the man who had helped her with her luggage coming toward them.

This was Kumar Ben Ari? *Sheikh* Kumar Ben Ari? Good Lord!

He and Mike met halfway. They threw their arms around each other and thumped each other's back.

"What in the hell took you so long?" Mike was saying as he led the other man to where Jenny and Josie waited.

"The line was long."

"But you've got a diplomatic passport. You could have gone ahead."

"Yes, well I . . ." He spotted Josie and his eyes widened with surprise before he laughed and said, "There was a most interesting distraction in the line next to me. A beautiful redhead who stopped me in my tracks." He gave Josie a mock salute, but before he could say anything else Jenny launched herself at him.

He picked her up and kissed both her cheeks. "Jenny!" he exclaimed. "How good it is to see you. I'm so happy for you and Mike. He's a lucky man." Still holding Jenny's hands, Kumar held her away from him. "But I'm not so sure how lucky you are. How are you going to keep a wild character like him in line?"

"With a smile and a bullwhip." She laughed and led him toward Josie. "This is my friend, Josie McCall," she said. "Josie, this is Kumar."

He took her hand and smiled. "We have met, after a fashion."

Josie didn't smile back. "Mr. Ben Ari helped me in the line with my bags," she said trying to hide her surprise, and yes, her chagrin at finding that the man she had thought so attractive a few minutes ago had turned out to be an Arabian friend of Mike and Jenny's. And that Jenny acted as though he were her best friend. Hadn't she had enough of Arabian men?

"Josie and I were in school together," Jenny told Kumar. "She works in Guatemala now." She put her arm around her friend and beamed up at her. "She's in charge of the International Health Organization there."

"You're a doctor?" Kumar asked.

Josie shook her head. "I have a master's in nursing, but my job is more administrative than medical." She turned away from him. "I suppose we can go now," she said to Mike.

When they had chatted in line she had been cordial and friendly, but for a reason Kumar didn't understand she wasn't being friendly now, which was strange because her friendship with Jenny and his with Mike should have smoothed the edges of their being strangers.

She was certainly attractive. With her flame red hair and wide, slightly tilted green eyes, she was a woman to turn any man's head.

When he had agreed to come to California to stand up for Mike he had expected to have a pleasant time. Jenny had told him on the phone all about her wonderful friend and he had been looking forward to meeting her. It was a delightful surprise to learn that the attractive woman in the immigration line was that friend. He could have sworn that she had found him as interesting as he'd found her, but now, for a reason he didn't understand, she had given a "back off, I'm not interested" signal. He was damned if he knew why.

"Okay," Mike said, breaking in on Kumar's thoughts. "Let's hit the road. It's almost a two-hour drive to Jenny's parents' ranch in Ramona. We'll stop in San Clemente for dinner if that's all right with the two of you."

He herded them toward the car, put their luggage in and held the door of the back seat for Josie and Kumar to enter.

Josie was disappointed. She'd been looking forward to coming to Jenny's wedding and she'd hoped that Mike's best man might be someone she'd have something in common with, a nice someone who would be her date at the rehearsal dinner as well as at the reception.

She was puzzled by Jenny's obvious affection for Kumar Ben Ari. After all she'd gone through with Aiden, how could she even look at another Middle Eastern man?

Eight years ago when Jenny had first told Josie she was going to marry Aiden Hurani, Josie had tried to warn her. They'd been sitting cross-legged on the floor of Josie's apartment in Berkeley sipping wine coolers, and Josie had said, "Look, Jen, I can understand the attraction. Aiden's a good-looking man. He's foreign and exotic and I suppose that's had a certain appeal for women ever since they swooned over Valentino in *The Sheik*. I'll admit that the idea of a dark desert type sweeping you up onto his horse and carrying you off into a Sahara sunset is fun to fantasize about. But that's all it is, a fantasy.

"Believe me when I tell you I know what I'm talking about," she'd gone on. "I know what Middle Eastern men are like. You should see the way the men in Il Hamaan treat their women. I was there as a medical person, but I couldn't do my job because I was a woman and as far as they were concerned, only good for one thing. That's why I asked for a transfer. That's why I'm butting in to try to talk you out of marrying Aiden."

But Jenny had been in love and nothing Josie said could sway her from her decision. The marriage had been a disaster. Aiden had beaten and abused Jenny, and she'd been a virtual prisoner in her own home. When at last she left him he had stolen their son and taken him out of Jenny's reach back to the desert country of his birth.

So yes, she thought again, I *am* prejudiced. But I can't help it. Jenny's my best friend and I know what she suffered. Kumar Ben Ari might be an incredibly attractive man, but he was, after all, a man like Aiden. She would be pleasant and reserved, and when the weekend was over she'd fly back to Guatemala and never have to think about him again.

The restaurant where they stopped overlooked the Pacific. It was the hour just after sunset and the sky still held that wonderful afterglow of red mingled with the gold of evening.

They ordered margaritas and the talk turned to the wedding.

"Rosa Hernandez is coming," Jenny said. "She and her new husband arrived yesterday. They're staying at a motel in San Diego. You and Kumar will stay at the ranch with us, of course." She took a sip of her margarita. "The wedding dinner and rehearsal is tomorrow night. The wedding's on Saturday."

The wedding talk continued through dinner. Josie wanted to know everything. "How many people have you invited?" she asked.

"Too many," Mike growled.

"A hundred and fifty," Jenny said.

"Where are you going on your honeymoon?"

"Tahiti," they said in unison.

"How many in the wedding party?"

"Eight and a half." Jenny smiled. "You and Kumar will stand up for us. Rosa, Marty and Sharon will be attendants and three of the men who work for Mike will be the ushers. Timmie's the half. He'll stand beside Kumar as a junior best man."

"Great kid." Mike bit into a piece of his steak. "A real trooper. After we grabbed him out of the Hurani house we got separated from Kumar and his men because of an *alize,* a sandstorm. It was tough going, but Timmie hung in there. I'm as crazy about him as I am about Jenny." He reached across the table and squeezed her hand. "Day after tomorrow both of you will belong to me, Jenny girl. I won't be able to relax until I know it's really happened. I still wake up at night and think it's all a dream. It scares the hell out of me that it won't come true."

"It'll come true," Jenny said softly. "All of our dreams will come true, Mike."

For a moment it was as though the two of them were alone in the restaurant. Kumar looked at Josie and when he saw the shine of tears in her eyes he had a sudden urge to reach out, as Mike had with Jenny, and take her hand.

She held his gaze, but only for the fraction of a second before she looked away.

Still holding Mike's hand, Jenny said, "I'd like to tell them our news, Mike. Is it all right? May I?"

He nodded. "If you want to, sweetheart."

She looked at Josie and Kumar. "Last week I found out that I'm pregnant." She blushed. "Both Mike and I realize it's somewhat before the fact, that it might have been better to wait until after we were married, but it happened and we're both pleased that it did. We hope the two of you will be, too."

Before Josie could say anything, Kumar got up and went around the table to Jenny and put his arms around her. "Thank you for telling us your wonderful secret," he said. He reached for Mike's hand. "Congratulations, my friend. I'm happy for you."

"Mike and I have talked about it," Jenny said when Kumar returned to his seat. "If the baby is a boy we'd like to name him Kumar. And we'd like you and Josie to be the godparents." Her smile took both of them in. "The two of you are our best friends, we want you to be a part of this."

"I'm most honored, Jenny." Kumar looked at Josie. "We are both honored, yes?"

"Yes," Josie said. "Of... of course. Congratulations. I'm happy for both of you."

Happy but surprised. Jen was her age. She still had time if she wanted more children. Why in the world had she chosen to get pregnant now? Or was she being a wet blanket, maybe even a little bit jealous because Jen had found someone to love who loved her and that together they were creating a new little person?

As though drawn by an invisible force, she looked up and saw Kumar watching her again—almost as if he knew what she had been thinking. For a moment she was held by his gaze, then she looked away and gave herself a mental shake. Of course she was happy for Jenny. Mike seemed like a nice guy. She hoped and prayed things worked out for them.

When they finished dinner they went to the car. It had been a long day and Josie was tired. When Kumar asked her about her life in Guatemala she said her work there was interesting, and not wanting to get into a conversation closed her eyes and leaned back against the seat.

The conversation drifted around her and she drowsed. Once, when they started into the mountains that led to Ramona, she was jostled against Kumar. Before she could move away he put an arm around her shoulder and brought her closer.

"You're tired," he said in a low voice. "Rest like this."

Josie pulled away, annoyed with him at taking the liberty, and with herself because she'd felt a sudden flutter of reaction at the touch of his thigh against hers. Reaction? Nonsense.

Nevertheless she sat up straighter, and though she was tired, did not close her eyes again.

Jenny's mother and father were waiting for them when they reached the ranch. Josie hugged Emily Cooper while Mike introduced Kumar to Jenny's father. Timmie had just gone to bed, Emily said, but very likely he was still awake and waiting for them.

"I'll go check on him," Jenny said, but before she could start for the house, Mike put a restraining hand on her arm.

"I'll do it," he told her. "Why don't you go in with Josie." He motioned to Kumar. "Come on up with me. Tim will be glad to see you again."

"It's become a nightly ritual," Jenny told them when they went into the house. "It's a special kind of man-to-man talking time. Mike's patient and loving with Timmie and I know he's going to be a terrific father."

"I was surprised about your being pregnant." Josie hesitated. "Well, not about your being pregnant, you know I'm happy for you, but maybe surprised that you announced it the way you did—in front of the Arabian, I mean."

"The Arabian?" Jenny frowned. "You make Kumar sound like a horse!" Her eyes flashed with anger. "Without his help, Mike and I might not have gotten out of Jahan alive. He's an exceptional man, and Mike and I are lucky to have him for a friend."

"You thought Aiden was a wonderful man, too."

"That's not fair. You're lumping all Middle Eastern men into one category. They're not all alike any more than all Americans or Irish or Italians are all alike. I'm surprised at you, Josie. This kind of prejudice isn't like you."

"I know what you went through in your marriage," Josie said quietly. "I know Aiden hurt you. I know you almost lost your son. And remember, Jenny, I lived in Il Hamaan for six months. Believe me when I tell you I know what Arabian men are like."

"But you don't know what Kumar's like." Jenny shook her head and with a disappointed look said, "I wanted so much for you and Kumar to get along. He's a great-looking man and I hoped you'd...you know, like each other.''

"Heaven forbid!" Josie said with a laugh. "The day I find myself falling for a desert sheikh is the day I head for the funny farm." She draped an arm over Jenny's shoulder. "Okay, Jen," she said, "I promise to behave. But if you've got any idea of teaming me up with your Sheikh Kumar Ben Ari you can forget it. This isn't my year for desert dudes."

He thought about her that night in bed and wondered why she had changed from the warm and friendly woman he'd first talked to at the airport into the coolly reserved woman she had become when she realized who he was. Surely she hadn't been offended by his joking remark about her being a gorgeous redhead. She *was* gorgeous.

He stretched his naked body under the sheet and thought about what it would be like to break through that cool reserve of hers. To have her smile at him, to touch his hand the way that Jenny had touched Mike's hand tonight.

He didn't have a monumental ego, but her obvious lack of interest pricked his male pride. He'd had more than his share of women, from the most beautiful dancing girls in half of Arabia to sophisticated French women, tall and lovely Scandinavians, brooding Russian models and lusty Italian beauties. He'd never thought of himself as a ladies' man, but in truth since he'd reached the age of puberty all he'd ever had to do was crook his finger at a woman.

He had a feeling that if he crooked his finger at Josie McCall, she'd laugh in his face. That annoyed the hell out of him.

He reached for a cigarette from the bedside table and lighted it. He had three days. If he couldn't change her mind about him in that length of time, he'd know that he'd definitely lost his touch.

But he would change her mind.

Through the drifting smoke from the cigarette he narrowed his eyes and saw her in his mind's eye, tall and elegant, the red hair pulled back off her face in the ladylike chignon, and that small sprinkling of freckles across her fair cheeks.

If she were his, he would loosen her hair so that it fell free about her bare shoulders, run his hands through it and feel it splayed across his chest. He'd kiss every one of her freckles and kiss her sweetly curved mouth. He would . . .

With a muttered curse, Kumar got out of bed and strode to the window. What in the hell was the matter with him? He didn't need to prove his masculinity to Josie McCall or any other woman. But dammit, there was something about her that heated his blood, something that made him want to make her lose that cool reserve, to make her mouth soften under his and her body tremble when he touched her.

He glared out the window, and as he took a long and bitter drag of the cigarette, his resolve firmed. Three days. If he didn't have Miss Josie McCall exactly where he wanted her by then, he'd check into the nearest clinic and see what ailed him.

He crushed the cigarette out and smiled. If Muhammad could move mountains, surely he could handle Josie McCall.

Chapter 2

"The three bridesmaids will come down the aisle with the three gentlemen," the Reverend John T. Porter said. "They'll be followed by the maid of honor, then by the bride and her father. The groom, the best man and the little fellow here—" he paused to pat the top of Timmie's head "—will be waiting at the altar." He motioned to the organist. "Let's try it, shall we?"

Josie had been in so many of her friends' weddings that she could do it by rote, but this wedding was special. Jenny was her best friend; she wanted everything to be beautiful for her.

When they reached the altar she gave Jenny a smile of encouragement, pantomimed taking the imaginary bouquet and moved to a position at Jenny's side.

The minister skimmed over most of what he would say. He finished with, "At this point I'll pronounce you man and wife and you may kiss your bride," and every-

body laughed when Mike actually did give Jenny a re-
sounding kiss before they started up the aisle.

Kumar took Josie's arm, as he would tomorrow at the
real wedding. "You are looking forward to the wedding, yes?"

Josie nodded. "Jen and I have been friends since college. I know what a tough time she had with that..." She
caught herself before she said, "that damn Arab," and
instead said, "with Aiden Hurani. Mike seems very nice
and it's obvious she's crazy about him."

"As he is about her." Kumar's voice grew serious.
"Never doubt that, Miss McCall. Mike loves Jenny with
all his heart."

She looked up at him, surprised and reassured at the
strength of his reply. When they reached the church
vestibule they stepped aside to make room for the other
couples coming down the aisle. Curious, she asked,
"Did you know Aiden?"

"Not Aiden, but I'd had a few business dealings with
his older brother, Mustafa. During the time I knew
Mustafa, Aiden was here in the United States going to
the university. I know from what Mike has told me that
Jenny had a difficult marriage, still I doubt that Aiden
was as bad as his brother. Mustafa was a dangerous
man. He would have cut out the heart of his grand-
mother if it served his purposes. He had a reputation
with women..." Kumar shook his head. "But no, it is
better not to say. It's over and he is dead."

"How did he die?"

"Mike killed him."

"Mike..." Her eyes widened in horror. "He killed
him?" She looked toward the man Jenny was going to
marry tomorrow. He was tall and powerfully built. Beside him Jenny looked small and defenseless.

"He is a good man," Kumar said, as though sensing her concern. "He loves Jenny, Miss McCall. Believe me when I tell you that your friend will always be safe with him."

Just at that moment Mike turned to speak to his bride-to-be and there came into his eyes an expression of such tenderness, such caring and love that Josie felt her eyes sting with tears. She turned to Kumar and said, "Thank you for reassuring me, Mr. Ben Ari."

"My name is Kumar." He held her gaze, and though his dark eyes were friendly, there was something behind them she couldn't quite define. She was caught by that look, unable to look away until he said, "The others are leaving. We must join them, yes?"

She ran her tongue nervously across her upper lip, and when she did, Kumar's eyes flared with sudden heat and he took a step forward.

"We...we have to leave," Josie said in a voice that did not sound like her own.

For a moment he only stood there, looking at her with his dark desert eyes. Then he took a deep breath and said, "Yes, of course. We don't want to keep them waiting, do we?"

She felt the pressure of his fingertips, and the word "Come," spoken in the accent that had so puzzled her at the airport.

Josie had given herself a talking-to after she had gone to bed the night before. Kumar was Jenny and Mike's friend; she wouldn't embarrass them because of her prejudice. She would be pleasant, even cordial, and the day after tomorrow she'd be on her way back to Guatemala.

But as she settled into the back seat of the car with Kumar for the drive to the hotel in San Diego where they would have the rehearsal dinner, she had to admit that there was something about him that disturbed, and yes, intrigued her.

All of the men, as well as the women, were elegantly turned out tonight, but Kumar stood out among them. He was as tall as Mike and he carried himself with quiet dignity and an almost old-world charm. If he were Spanish he would have been a count, if English surely a duke. But he wasn't, he was an Arabian prince, a sheikh of the desert, in a world she did not like.

The caravan of three cars made the fifty-mile drive to the Hotel Del Coronado in a little less than an hour. And though she chatted and joked, all the way there Josie was very aware of Kumar beside her in the back seat. He kept his distance, but once or twice on the curving road that led to the main highway she was jostled against him. Each time that happened she felt a tingle of something she couldn't quite explain.

Okay, she told herself. So he's an attractive man, different from anyone I've ever known, and that in itself is a little exciting. Then, too, there's the whirl and romance of the wedding festivities, and the age-old cliché of the maid of honor and the best man being attracted to each other. That's all it is. I'm letting myself get caught up in the excitement of the wedding.

They arrived at the hotel on the beach just as the sun was setting over the Pacific. It was a rambling Victorian-style hotel that faced the sea. Built when Grover Cleveland was president, the Hotel Del Coronado had entertained princes and presidents, Marilyn Monroe and business moguls. It was charming and romantic, the perfect place for a rehearsal dinner.

There were fourteen of them at a long table overlooking the sea. Kumar ordered champagne, and when it came and they were served, he stood, raised his glass and began to speak in Arabic.

Only Mike and Jenny nodded in understanding. Their faces grew serious and Josie saw Mike swallow hard. When Kumar had finished he said, "Thank you, my friend."

Kumar nodded and, in English, translated: "In the whisper of the wind, the voices of Muhammad and of God and all his angels mingle and become one in this joyous celebration of a man and a woman who are about to be joined in marriage." He smiled at Mike, then at Jenny. "The two of you have been fortunate enough to have found love," he went on. "Cherish and sustain that love. Wake each morning with joyous hearts at the gladness of the day, and sleep at night in the warmth and comfort of each other's arms."

He turned to the others. "Let us raise our glasses to our friends and wish them well."

"Hear, hear," Jenny's father said. "To Mike and Jenny. A lifetime of happiness."

Josie reached across the table and clasped Jenny's hand. "Happiness always, dear Jen," she whispered.

More champagne was poured, more toasts were offered. Day faded into a lingering twilight, an orchestra began to play. Mike took Jenny's hand, kissed it and led her to the place where a few other couples were dancing.

Kumar stood and came around the table. Josie turned to smile up at him. She even started to push back her chair, when he paused at the chair next to hers and asked, "May I have this dance, Sharon?"

"Love to," Sharon said.

When they came back to the table he asked Marty to dance, then Rosa, then Sharon again. By the time dinner was served Josie had lost her appetite. This is dumb, she told herself, but damm it all, she was the maid of honor. Out of common courtesy, Kumar should have asked her to dance. Jenny's father did, and so did two of the ushers. Kumar, however, seemed to have forgotten she was even there.

But when the after-dinner drinks were served he got up, and coming around the table to the back of her chair, said, "Please, will you dance with me, Miss McCall?"

If he hadn't already pulled her chair out, she would have refused. But he had, and there was very little she could do except offer her hand.

The glittering lights of the crystal chandeliers had dimmed. The voices of the diners were muted. A black woman with a silky, sultry voice began to sing with the orchestra.

Kumar put his arms around her, and though at first Josie moved reluctantly into his embrace, she soon found herself forgetting her earlier mood and moving with him to the strains of "Besame Mucho."

He was a good dancer, smooth, confident. He tucked one of her hands against his chest, and when he urged her closer, she could feel the slight ripple of muscle under the hand that rested against his shoulder. In her three-inch heels she was almost as tall as he was. The line of his hip matched hers, their shoulders were level, their faces almost touching.

We're a perfect fit, she found herself thinking. Here was a man she didn't have to wear small heels or flat heels with, as she had in high school and later in college. She smiled, remembering that whenever a friend had wanted to fix her up with a young man her first question had always been, "How tall is he?" Later, as she had matured, the question of height hadn't bothered her. She'd dated men who were shorter, but she'd never felt really comfortable dancing with a man who came just to her shoulder.

"The Way We Were" segued into "Yesterday," then "Evergreen." "Lost inside of you..." the singer sang.

Josie felt the slight pressure of Kumar's hand bringing her closer so that her cheek touched his. She had the fleeting thought that this wasn't a good idea and that she'd better move out of his embrace. And she would. In a minute or two.

Her breath was warm against his cheek, her body slim and graceful against his. He hadn't asked her to dance earlier, partly to prove to himself that he wasn't all that attracted to her and partly to show her that he did not find her any more attractive than the other women in the wedding party.

But he did find her attractive. Tonight she had worn a pale pink dress that was gathered and beaded at the waist. With her red hair pulled back off her face and just a touch of makeup she was astonishingly beautiful. He stepped a little away so that he could look at her. Her lips curved in the beginning of a smile and it was all he could do not to kiss her right here on the dance floor.

Yesterday her antipathy toward him had been painfully apparent, and though today she had been courteous, he could still sense an underlying feeling of aloofness. It was almost as if she were holding her hands up in front of her and saying she wanted nothing to do with him.

He had asked her to dance to prove to himself that he could sway her. But it was he who had been swayed, he who felt this sudden surge of desire. He wanted to kiss her until her lips quivered and parted under his, wanted to touch the high, firm breasts that pressed so enticingly against his chest. He wanted...

The music stopped. Kumar took a deep breath and let her go. Her hand still rested on his shoulder, her mouth looked soft and vulnerable. He looked at her for a long moment, and because he could not help himself, he touched her face.

Her skin was soft and warm, her eyes were luminous. He ran the tips of his fingers across the fullness of her lips and felt them quiver under his touch. He whispered her name, "Josie?" before he stepped back, and taking her hand, led her back to the others.

She felt as if she had been drugged. As if she'd had too much wine. She didn't walk back to the table, she floated, still lost in the magic of the music. And in the touch of his hand so gently caressing her face.

The others were standing, ready to leave. Mike motioned him aside. "Would you mind driving Josie back to the ranch?" he asked. "Jenny's father is a little under the weather and I think I should drive his car." He handed Kumar his keys. "Sure you don't mind?"

Kumar's lips twitched. "Of course not. We'll see you back at the ranch."

He took Josie's arm and they followed the others out of the hotel. He thought she looked a little nervous, but she didn't say anything. When Mike's car was delivered, he helped her in and said, "You're the guide. Without you I will be completely lost."

She gave him directions. And sat over as far as she could on her side of the car, disturbed and a little annoyed that she had let herself get carried away by the music. Love songs, she thought disparagingly, sweet sentimental stuff that had lovers swooning in each other's arms. The next time Kumar asked her to dance she hoped the orchestra was playing rap.

They took the Coronado Bridge and from the top span they could see all the lights of San Diego, the bay and the ocean beyond. It was a beautiful night, clean and clear with just the slightest nip in the air that warned of cooler days to come.

Nervous because she was alone with Kumar in the dark closeness of the car, Josie felt as if she had to say something. And so she said, "Tell me about...I'm sorry, I've forgotten where it is that you're from."

"Abdu Resaba." He turned to glance at her. "It's a small country, probably no larger than your states of Connecticut and Massachusetts if they were linked together. Only a portion of the country is on the Mediterranean, that is where the city of Bir Chegga is located."

"And where you live?"

Kumar nodded. "The rest of the country is desert and oil wells. So though we are small, we're among the top five oil-producing countries in the world. We have some seven million people, most of whom are Muslims. The Bedouins and the Berbers adopted the Islamic religion in the eighth century, when the first Arabs entered the country."

He turned to her. "Most Westerners know very little about Middle Eastern countries, with the exception of Egypt perhaps. It's a remarkable country. Have you ever been there?"

Josie shook her head. "My only experience with the Middle East has been in Il Hamaan."

"Il Hamaan?" He sounded surprised. "When were you there?"

"Eight years ago. It was my first assignment for International Health. I didn't like it."

"I should think not. It's really a very backward country. The customs there are archaic."

"What about the customs in Abdu Resaba? I thought all Middle Eastern countries were the same."

"Of course they aren't. Abdu Resaba is nothing like Il Hamaan."

"Aren't the women in your country, like the women in Jahan and Il Hamaan, veiled? Aren't they considered second-class citizens?"

"Second-class citizens?" Kumar frowned, and tightened his hands on the steering wheel. "Our women are treated with the utmost honor and respect. We treasure and guard them."

"Guard them?" Josie asked. "You mean you hide them behind their robes and their veils, don't you?"

Kumar bristled. "We protect them. There's a difference. We believe that a woman must not show either her body or her face to anybody other than her husband and close relatives. That is done not because we consider them of a lower station, but because we love them. They are as free as we are. They have professions, as we do, and in the last few years many of them have become lawyers and teachers."

"But they still wear the veil."

"Of course they do, when they're out on the street or meeting with strangers."

"Because men say they have to. Because men run the country and because, no matter what you say, women *are* second-class citizens."

"No," he said, getting angry. "You don't understand."

"I understand all right," she muttered under her breath, and after that she didn't speak except to tell him where to turn and which highway exit to take.

At last they turned into the private road that led to the ranch. When they did, Kumar pulled to the side of the road and turned off the ignition.

"What are you doing?" Josie glared at him. "Why are you stopping?"

"You were being judgmental before," he said. "You had a bad experience in one country and so you see fit to judge Abdu Resaba without knowing anything about it. You criticize something you don't understand."

"I understand all right. I understand countries that are run by a lot of chauvinistic males."

He turned on the seat to face her. "Ours is a centuries-old culture, Miss McCall. We adhere to the old ways, the old customs. I assure you that we hold our women in the highest esteem. If that means not wanting them to walk around in the kind of ten-inch skirts some of your women wear and exposing themselves to every male eye, then yes, we are a chauvinistic society."

His eyes grew dark with anger. "We believe that what is between a man and a woman is something wonderful and special, not to be shared by others." He leaned closer. "If I loved a woman I would protect her, and yes, I, too, would shield her from any eyes except mine."

"You'd make her wear a robe and a veil and hide her behind great stone walls." Josie shook her head. "You're a chauvinist, Kumar, probably the biggest chauvinist in Ali Baba or whatever that place you're from is called."

"Abdu Resaba." He took a deep breath and tried to speak calmly. "You don't understand our culture. Perhaps you're right in saying that we're chauvinistic, but that is because we are the stronger sex and we know what is best for our women better than they do. We love them, and because we do, we care for them as though they were precious jewels, or children who must be guided in the ways..." He stopped as Josie opened the door. "What are you doing?"

She didn't bother to answer. She simply got out of the car and started up the road toward the house.

He smacked the steering wheel and swore an ancient Bedouin curse before he got out of the car and hurried after her. By Allah, this woman tried his patience!

He caught up with her, took her arm and turned her around. "This is ridiculous," he said. "Get back in the car."

"I'd rather walk."

"I'd rather you didn't."

She tried to pull away, but he tightened his grip on her arm. "Just because you don't agree with the customs of my country is no reason why you should be angry. You're acting like a spoiled child."

"Or like a woman," she said furiously.

He took a step closer. "The most aggravating, the most opinionated woman I've ever met." He gripped her arms. "I'd like to take you home with me so that you could see for yourself how a proper woman behaves."

"Thanks, but no thanks, Valentino. It'd be a cold day in hell before I'd even set foot in your country."

He said something she didn't understand but knew was probably an oath, and before she could move away he pulled her into his arms and covered her mouth with his.

For a moment she was too startled to protest. When she did, she tried to get away. But his arms tightened around her and his mouth moved hard against hers.

She smacked his shoulders with the flat of her hands, but he wouldn't let her go. Furious at being held this way against her will, she continued to struggle. But hard as she tried he wouldn't release her.

The kiss was angry, demanding. She pressed her lips tightly together and when she did he ran his tongue across them and nipped the corners of her mouth before he trailed a path of moist kissing bites down the line of her throat.

His breath was hot, his tongue seared her skin. He came back to find her mouth again, and his mouth was hard and insistent against hers.

She fought against him. And God help her, against the flame that warmed and excited.

"Kiss me back," he murmured against her lips. "Kiss me the way I want you to, Josie."

He pronounced it "Sho-zee." Seductively. Softly. Coaxing a response she didn't want to give. But at last, as if of their own volition, her lips parted and softened under his.

"Yes," he whispered, and there was triumph in his voice. "This is what I wanted. This is the way I knew it would be."

He touched his tongue to hers and it was as if a thousand volts of electricity went off inside her. She tried to resist, but tentatively, slowly, her tongue touched his.

He sighed against her lips and brought her closer into his embrace, no longer holding her as if she were a prisoner, but with strength and tenderness.

She was on fire, every nerve ending alive as sensation after sensation coursed through her. His mouth was so warm. He tasted her. He licked her lips, nipped and suckled them. She felt his heat. And her own.

He put a hand against the small of her back and she felt him hard against the thin fabric of her dress.

She moaned low in her throat and knew from his whispered response that the sound excited him. He drew her even closer. White heat flamed through her body and the flame he had kindled snaked down, burning a path of pure fire, making her go weak with longing.

He held her there and began to move against her in a touch so intimate she cried out. He took her cry and his arms tightened around her. The kiss deepened. He wouldn't let her go.

A sob rose in her throat. She was frantic with desire, desperate in her need to be closer, closer.

"Sho-zee," he whispered. "Sho-zee."

He cupped a breast, and when he ran his thumb across her nipple, she trembled and tried to move away.

"No, stay," he pleaded. "Let me touch you this way." He held her with his hand and caressed her with his fingertips. He ran his nails across the peak and she swayed against him, weak with desire.

He murmured words she did not know or understand against her lips. Arabic words. Arabic...

Dear God... With every bit of her strength, Josie pulled away from him. Her heart was beating hard against her ribs, her breath came in painful gasps. She looked at him. His dark eyes were narrowed, hot with passion.

He said "Josie?" and held out his hand to her.

"No," she whispered. "Oh, no," and with a cry she turned and ran toward the house.

Kumar didn't move. He watched her go, clenched hands to his sides, and took deep, painful breaths to try to ease the terrible ache in his body. A shudder ran through him. "Josie," he said aloud. "Come back."

But the only sound he heard was the whisper of the wind through the cottonwood trees.

"If you were mine..." He spoke the words aloud. A smile that was not altogether pleasant crossed his face. If Josie McCall were his...if she were in his country, in Abdu Resaba...

The thought hung suspended in the soft night air and an idea began to form.

He was smiling when he got back into the car and drove slowly toward the ranch.

Chapter 3

The day of the wedding dawned bright and clear. Though Josie knew what an exciting day lay ahead, she did not want to move from her bed. She had slept fitfully. Every time she'd drifted to sleep, thoughts of Kumar Ben Ari had stirred her to wakefulness. When at last she did sleep, it was to dream strange, erotic dreams of him....

Kumar against the backdrop of hot desert sands, in tight, white riding breeches and flowing shirt, legs apart in a threatening stance. A riding crop in one hand, beckoning to her with the other....

Kumar astride a black stallion, racing across the desert toward her. She ran in slow motion, feet sinking into the sand, legs refusing her command to go faster... faster. The sound of hoofbeats thundering after her, a hand reaching out for her....

In his arms, pressed close to his body. Her heart beating wildly in her breast. His arms strong around her. The heat of his body warming her. The movement of a black stallion beneath them as they raced together across the desert sands. Toward—

She had been trembling when she awakened, her body heated with strange desires. Now, tired and out of sorts, she propped herself up on the bed pillows and glared into the room. A man had kissed her and she had responded. It didn't mean anything. She'd had too much champagne. It had been a mistake, but it wouldn't happen again. As for her dreams...

"Josie?" There was a light tap on the door. "Josie, are you awake?"

"Sure, Jen. Come in."

"I can't. I've got a tray."

"Hold on." Josie scrambled out of bed and hurried to the door, and when she opened it Jenny came in.

"Everybody else is still asleep. I thought we could have coffee and talk. I'm...maybe a little nervous."

"That's understandable." Josie took the tray and put it on the table by the window. "Coffee and chocolate doughnuts sprinkled with nuts." She sniffed the familiar aroma and grinned. "Just like old times."

Jenny sat down and pulled the robe more tightly around her against the early morning California chill. "I needed the chance to be alone with you for a little while," she said. "I keep thinking about the first time I got married. You were my maid of honor then, too." She put a dollop of cream in her coffee. "I expected so much, Joze, and I got so little."

Josie reached across the table and took Jenny's hand. "It will be different this time. Mike's not like Aiden. He's a good man and he loves you." She squeezed Jenny's hand before she released it. "And he's your own kind, Jen. This time you know who you're marrying."

Jenny smiled. "I really do love him. He acts tough and talks tough, but I know the kind of man he is." She took a sip of her coffee. "I've missed you, Josie. I wish you weren't so faraway."

"So do I." Josie bit into a doughnut, said, "Umm, that's so good!" and dabbed at a bit of chocolate at the corner of her mouth. "I like Guatemala, Jen, and I love the people and the work I do. I've managed to staff and set up small clinics all around the countryside. We immunize children and adults against malaria and tuberculosis, talk to young women about birth control, to *everybody* about AIDS, do minor surgeries, treat gunshot wounds—"

"Gunshot..." Jenny's eyes widened. "You're kidding!"

Josie shook her head. "No, I'm not. Things aren't as bad as they were a few years ago, but there's still the occasional skirmish, sometimes close to the clinics."

"But that's dangerous! You could be killed."

"Not likely. It's better than it was when I first went there." She took another bite of her doughnut. "Besides, I may not be there too much longer. There's been talk of a promotion, that maybe I'm next in line to be head of either the Washington or the Paris office."

"Paris! That would be great."

"Yes, wouldn't it? I'd miss the nursing part, but actually I do very little of that now because I'm in more of a supervisory position. I have a feeling it's time for a change, and I'm crossing my fingers on Paris." She smiled at her friend. "What about you, Jen. Where will you and Mike live?"

"We've bought a small ranch just outside of Las Vegas. It'll be a good place to raise children. Mike and I want at least one more." She patted her stomach. "After this one, I mean."

"You're really crazy about him, aren't you?" Josie smiled. "So why are you nervous?"

"Wedding jitters. The excitement of everything, wondering if my hair will be all right, if Mike will like my gown. But no doubts at all about how I feel about him." She took another sip of her coffee. "Now what about you?" she asked. "How's your love life?"

"What love life? I've been too busy the last couple of years to even think about a man."

"Oh?" Jenny shot her a speculative look, and with studied nonchalance, said, "What do you think about Kumar? Now that you know him a little better, I mean."

"He's..." Josie hesitated. "All right," she said carefully.

"All right? Come on! Kumar is one of the best-looking men I've ever met!" She leaned forward. "I've seen the way he looks at you. I'd bet my wedding garter that he's attracted to you."

"Well, I'm not attracted to him!" Josie frowned at her coffee. "I'll admit he's a good-looking man. But I'm not interested. Okay?"

Jenny sighed. "I'd been kinda hoping you would be. Kumar's been a wonderful friend to Mike and to me. He's loyal and true, brave, fearless—"

"Oh, come *on*, Jen. You're making him sound like a superhero!"

Jenny's blue eyes flashed. "He is a super *nice* hero. Next to Mike, he's one of the finest men I know."

"Okay!" Josie held her hands up in surrender. "Okay, okay. So he's wonderful. I get the picture. But that doesn't mean he appeals to me, because he doesn't."

But even as she said it, Josie knew it wasn't true. Last night when Kumar kissed her, it had been explosive enough to set the California redwoods on fire. She'd never been kissed like that before, had never responded to anyone with that kind of passion. And that, she supposed, had scared the hell out of her.

"Look," she said, "you know how I feel about Middle Eastern men. I honestly don't think mixed marriages work, not with any nationality, but especially with men like Aiden and Kumar. You've seen it yourself, Jen. You know what Aiden put you through. As for me, I'd join a convent before I ever got mixed up with a man like that."

"Kumar's different."

"No, he isn't. We talked last night when we were driving back here. I asked him about the women in his country, and he's all for their being robed and veiled. He admitted he's a chauvinist and he actually said that men were the stronger sex and that *they* make the decisions because they know what's best for their women." Josie shook her head. "Uh uh," she said. "A man like Kumar Ben Ari is strictly off-limits."

The wedding began at four. Though this was Jenny's second marriage she had wanted it to be a big one, and it was. She wore a gown of ivory satin trimmed with chantilly lace and tiny seed pearls. Instead of a veil she wore a scattering of seed-pearl petals in her hair.

The men, even Timmie, wore tails. The three bridesmaids' dresses were daffodil yellow and Josie's gown was the same shade of green as her eyes.

Kumar watched her as she came down the aisle ahead of Jenny. Instead of the chignon, she wore her hair soft about her shoulders. Small green orchids were scattered through it. She looked like a forest princess, so beautiful she took his breath.

He remembered how she had felt in his arms last night, and how, for too brief a moment, she had responded to him. Anger and desire mingled as he watched her take her place opposite him. She kept her eyes lowered and did not look at him.

He had never been to a Christian wedding before. Jenny was not veiled as the brides were in his country. Only at the end of his people's ceremony would the veil be lifted by the groom as if, as it had been in the customs of old, he were looking upon the face of his bride for the first time.

He didn't understand western customs or the freedom given to women here. As any man would, he appreciated a woman's beauty, her face and form. And yes, when he was in the West he, too, turned his head to admire a nice pair of legs shown off to such advantage by a miniskirt. But he would have been appalled and angered, as would any man of his country, by the sight of a Middle Eastern woman behaving in such a manner.

Though he had gone to school in the West and had traveled extensively, he had never become accustomed to western ways or western women. They were too opinionated, too independent. He still remembered the first time he'd sat in on a political discussion at Princeton, how appalled he'd been when the girl he'd been dating began to argue a point with him.

He simply did not understand western women. Nor did he understand the men who did not want to shield and protect them from all other eyes except their own. Did western men not know what joy there was in slowly undressing a woman who belonged to you, to know that no other but you had looked upon her exquisite face and form?

When he married it would be to such a woman, a woman of his own kind, whom no other male eyes had gazed upon. She would be pure in every sense of the word, quiet, not given to argument or raising her voice to give an unasked for opinion. She would be . . .

"May I have the ring?" the minister said.

Timmie nudged him and Kumar, startled out of his thoughts, took the ring the little boy gave him. He handed it to Mike and watched as Mike took Jenny's left hand in his.

"With this ring and with my heart I pledge my love for you," Mike said as he slipped the plain gold band on Jenny's finger.

Josie handed Jenny the ring she had placed on her own finger so that she wouldn't lose it.

Jenny took Mike's hand. "And with this ring, with my heart and my soul, with everything that is in me, I, too, pledge my love," she whispered.

Clasping hands, the bride and groom looked into each other's eyes. And Josie felt, mingled with her happiness for her friend, an emptiness within her own heart, and yes, a longing for someone to love her as Mike loved Jenny. Tears glistened in her eyes and she bowed her head so no one would see as the minister began to speak the solemn, yet joyful words uniting Mike and Jenny as man and wife.

The organ pealed a triumphant chord. Mike kissed his new bride amid heartfelt applause, and when he released her they started back down the aisle.

Instead of taking Josie's arm, Kumar reached for her hand and clasped it in his as they followed Mike and Jenny.

"You weep," he said in a low voice. "May I ask why?"

Josie took a deep breath to steady herself. "I . . . I always cry at weddings," she managed to say.

He tightened his hand on hers. She looked up at him and when he saw the tears still glistening on her eyelashes, he said, "Your eyes are the color of the waters of the Nile."

She tried to slip her hand from his, but he wouldn't let her go.

"Beautiful women should only weep for gladness, never for sadness," he said.

"I'm not sad," Josie protested. "My tears were tears of happiness for Mike and Jenny."

"I see." His smile was gentle, unbelieving.

They reached the vestibule, but still he did not let her go. The others in the party were gathered around Mike and Jenny. Voices were raised, there was laughter and good cheer, embraces, congratulations.

Kumar held Josie back, and in the same softly compelling voice, asked, "Is there someone special in your life, Miss McCall?"

Josie looked at him, taken aback by the personal question. "We really must join the others," she said.

"Is there someone?" he persisted.

She shook her head. "I've been far too busy for that. My job is important to me. I don't have the time for anything else."

He took the hand he had been holding and brought it to his lips. Before Josie could protest he turned it so that he could kiss her palm. His lips were warm, soft. She felt the barest touch of his tongue against her skin.

She stared at him, shocked at the intimacy of the gesture, and pulled her hand away. She went to embrace

Jenny and to kiss Mike's cheek. "Congratulations," she said. "I'm so happy for both of you."

And tried not to see the speculative look in Kumar Ben Ari's dark desert eyes when he, too, congratulated the bride and groom.

The wedding reception was held at the ranch. A tent big enough to accommodate all the guests had been erected on the lawn, along with tables and chairs, a buffet that would have satisfied the most profound gourmet and pink champagne that bubbled from a crystal fountain. Instead of an orchestra, a mariachi band played at one end of the rolling lawn.

Kumar was seated next to Josie at the bridal table. Toasts were given amid laughter and a few tears. When Timmie asked his mother, "Why can't I go with you and Mike to Tahooti?" only Kumar and Jenny were close enough to hear.

"Tahiti," Mike said, drawing the boy to him. "The next time your mom and I go somewhere you'll come along, but this is a honeymoon trip, Tim. It's a special time for a husband and wife to... well, to sorta get acquainted."

"But you and Mom are already acquainted." Tim looked puzzled. "Aren't you?"

"Mike means getting acquainted as man and wife." Jenny ruffled her son's hair. "We'll only be gone two weeks, Tim, and when we come back the three of us will move into our very own house."

"With Ralph," Timmie said.

"Hell of a name for a horse." Mike grinned and nodded. "Yeah, partner, with Ralph."

As Josie watched the exchange, any fears she might have had about Jenny's happiness vanished. Mike was a rare man, and Jenny was lucky to have found him. They would be, along with Timmie and the child they were to have, a loving family, and she rejoiced for them.

When a few of the couples moved from the tent and wandered out onto the lawn where the mariachis played, Mike rose, and taking Jenny's hand, led her to a smooth patch of lawn under the trees and drew her into his arms.

He and Jenny were so perfect together, Josie thought as she watched them. He was tall, more rugged than handsome, even in his white tie and tails. The top of Jenny's head just reached his shoulder. He held her gently, as if she were a fragile doll that might break at the slightest touch. And once again Josie felt reassured, for surely here was a man who would, unlike Aiden, love and protect her friend.

A few of the other couples began to dance, and afraid that Kumar might ask her, Josie started to back away. But before she could, Kumar took her hand and said, "Come, let us walk a bit."

If she didn't want to make a scene, she had no choice but to let him take her away from the others.

In a conversational tone, he said, "You look very beautiful today, Josie."

Her name sounded as strange on his lips as it had last night. "Sho-zee," softer somehow than Josie.

"It was a nice wedding, yes? I'm happy for Mike. Jenny is a wonderful woman. She will make Mike a good wife, a good mother to his children."

"And *her* children."

He looked surprised. "Of course."

"Are you married, Prince Ben Ari?"

"No."

"Have you ever been?"

He shook his head. "But I am thirty-six. Soon I must think about it." He glanced at her and his lips twitched in a smile. "According to our beliefs we are allowed four wives. If I am to have four I should begin collecting them soon."

Josie's lips tightened. "And what will you do with four wives, Prince?" she asked, with a hard emphasis on the word *prince*.

Kumar pretended to think. "Let me see," he said, stroking his chin. "One will cook, one will take care of the many children I will have, another will manage the household. And the fourth wife..." He lifted his shoulders. "Ah, she will be special, for she will be the one who takes care of me."

Josie gave an unladylike snort, and when she did Kumar laughed. "I'm teasing," he said. "One woman is enough for any man." He tugged at her hand. "Come, let us walk toward the barn. I want to see Timmie's colt."

And because she felt a little foolish at having been taken in by his joking, if indeed he had been joking, Josie didn't protest.

It was a beautiful day. The meadows were filled with clover, wild roses and lavender daisies. Trees bordered the property of the ranch, white oak, ponderosa pine, willows and pepper trees that dipped low over the stream that trickled down from the mountains.

The music of the mariachis drifted down to them, but other than that there was only the occasional song of a bird.

Kumar led Josie to a shady spot under one of the pepper trees. Leaning back against the gnarled trunk, he asked, "When do you return to Guatemala?"

"Tomorrow evening." She hesitated. "When is your flight?"

"In the morning. Mike's father is driving me to the airport."

"You go to New York, then Paris and home?"

Kumar shook his head. "No, I'm flying to Washington."

"Washington?" She sounded surprised.

He nodded. "I have diplomatic business there."

"I see." She had almost forgotten that he was the acting head of his country, and she found it strange that she was standing here with him on this sunny afternoon in southern California, with the breeze gentle on her face and the sound of the mariachi music drifting on the autumn air.

"I would like to see you again," he said.

Josie looked at him, startled. "That's hardly possible. I mean..." She shrugged. "I live in Guatemala and you're on the other side of the world."

"I could arrange for you to visit my home."

"I don't think so."

He pushed himself away from the tree and moved closer. "Why did you run away from me last night?"

She took a deep breath before she answered. "You shouldn't have kissed me," she said. "I shouldn't have let you. It was the champagne. It was—"

"No." He took her face between his hands. "It wasn't the champagne, Josie. It was you and me and a wonderful magic that happened between us when we kissed. That's why I want to see you again."

"Please, let me go."

"Not until you tell me why you ran away from me last night."

His face was only inches from hers. Before she could free herself he kissed her. She tried not to respond, but his mouth roamed so hungrily, so knowingly over hers, and when he said, "Open your lips for me, kiss me as I am kissing you," her lips parted under his.

It was a little like being lost in a vast and empty space, where only his arms could protect her. With his thumbs he stroked her closed eyes, her cheeks, the corners of her mouth.

The kiss deepened when he pressed past her lips to seek her tongue. He drew her closer and she heard the catch of his breath.

"Don't you feel it?" he whispered against her lips. "Don't you feel the magic that happens when we kiss?"

His mouth roamed over hers. She felt herself slipping over the edge of reality and knew that in another moment she would be lost.

"Josie," he said. "Sho-zee."

She pulled away from him. "No!" she said, breathing hard. "No!" She held her hands up in front of her and backed away.

"What is it? What's wrong?"

"I don't want to do this." The words came half strangled from her throat. "I don't!"

"But what are you afraid of? Do you think that because you live in one country and I in another that we will never see each other again after today? That for me this is . . . what do you say? A flirtation? A romantic excitement because of our friends' wedding?" He rested a hand on her shoulder. "I believe you know it is more than that."

"I don't want it to be more."

"But why?"

"Because I know about men like you," she said.

"Men like me? What do you mean?"

"Middle Eastern men. I know what you're like. I know what you think about women."

"I adore women." He smiled and reached for her.

She stepped back. "I know what happened to Jenny. I know how Aiden abused her."

"But I'm not Aiden."

"You're like him."

"How do you know that?"

"I know."

His expression changed, hardened. "I see. Then there can be nothing between us. Is that what you're saying?"

"That's it." She felt stronger now, more in control. "I'm sorry, Kumar. I don't mean to be rude. But no, there can be nothing between us."

"You have made up your mind. Yes?"

She took a steadying breath. "Yes," she said firmly.

He shrugged, but there was a glint of danger in his eyes when he said, "Very well. Shall we go back to the others?"

He didn't touch her or take her hand. When they reached the tent he left her, and in a little while she went back to the house with Jenny to help her change into her traveling suit.

When Jenny was ready, they came downstairs to find the wedding guests had gathered and were waiting for them.

"Throw your bouquet, dear," her mother said.

"I will." But first Jenny hugged Josie. "Thank you for coming," she said. "Thank you for standing up with me."

Josie tightened her arms around her. "Happiness, Jen," she whispered. "Now and always." Then she ran quickly down the stairs and moved to the back of the single women who waited to catch the bridal bouquet.

When it was tossed, she made no attempt to catch it. But it bounced off the raised arm of the woman next to her and when she tried to deflect it she somehow ended up holding it.

She heard the cries of congratulations and turned to see Jenny laughing down at her. Josie shook her head, laughing with Jen. But the laughter died on her lips when she turned and saw Kumar. He wasn't laughing.

Jenny's father drove Kumar to the airport the following morning.

"Off to Washington?" the older man asked when he stopped in front of the terminal.

"Yes, I have some business there." Kumar got out of the car, and when he had taken his bags, shook Mr. Cooper's hand. "Thank you for bringing me here," he said. "It was very kind of you."

"You're Mike's best friend, Mr. Ben Ari. We all appreciate your coming so far to be in the wedding."

"It was my pleasure, I assure you."

The driver behind Cooper's car blew his horn. "Goodbye," Kumar said. "Thank you again."

He watched Jenny's father drive off. Then he picked up his suitcase and headed into the terminal. Four days ago when he had come to California, it had not been his intention to go to Washington. But he had changed his plans; he had something very important to attend to in that city.

Chapter 4

"How good it is to see you again." James T. Harwood, under secretary of foreign relations, motioned Kumar to a chair across from his desk. "How long has it been? A year?"

"More like two." Kumar grinned. "The dancing girls at the Palais Royale ask about you every time I go in."

"Which is often, I suppose," Harwood said with a laugh.

"Of course. There is one girl in particular who actually has tears in her eyes when she asks when you will return. Jemena? Yes, that's the one. The last time I saw her she said, 'When will your friend, the tall man with the gray eyes and the beautiful mouth return?'"

"The beautiful mouth. Did she really say that?" Harwood sighed. "Jemena. God, what a beautiful girl. Voluptuous, creative, exciting..." The man shook his head. "Don't tempt me, Kumar. The thought of her makes me want to get on the first plane to Abdu Resaba.''

"Can't you manage a trip?"

"Not any time soon, but . . ." Harwood tapped long, slender fingers on the top of his desk. "Tell you what, I've got a trip scheduled for Saudi in four or five months. As soon as I've finished with my business there, I'll come to Abdu Resaba."

"Good. Let me know and I'll arrange a hunting trip into the desert. But first we will spend a few nights in the Palais Royale, yes?"

"Yes! Tell Jemena I'm coming, will you? And be sure she has no other . . . uh, appointments that week."

"Of course. I'll arrange it."

"Can you have dinner with me tonight? I know a couple of stunning young ladies who would be only too happy to have dinner with us."

"Dinner, yes. But perhaps this time we will dine alone if you don't mine."

"Very well. Shall we say eight at your hotel?" Harwood reached for a cigar. "Anything I can do for you while you're in Washington?"

"Yes, as a matter of fact there is. I'd like to meet the head of the International Health Organization here in Washington. If you could arrange an appointment, I'd be most appreciative."

"No problem. Fellow by the name of Ron Marshall is in charge. His office is in the other wing. If he's not busy he can be here in a few minutes."

"Splendid," Kumar said.

Harwood picked up the phone and spoke to a secretary on the other end. "Prince Kumar Ben Ari of Abdu Resaba is in my office," he said. "He'd like to see Mr.

Marshall, right away if it's possible." He nodded. "Ten minutes? Yes, that's fine."

Kumar leaned back in his chair, and with a satisfied smile, lighted a cigarette.

Ten minutes later Harwood's secretary ushered Ron Marshall in. He was several inches taller than Harwood, younger, perhaps in his early forties, with an Ichabod Crane thinness. He greeted Kumar effusively, all but clicking his heels as he bowed and said, "Prince Kumar! What an honor. Is there anything, anything at all we can do for you?"

"Yes," Kumar said, "as a matter of fact there is. We in Abdu Resaba are badly in need of your help."

He motioned Marshall to a chair and the thin man sat, knees together, feet apart, an expectant and somewhat worried look on his face. "How can we be of assistance, Mr.... uh, Prince Ben Ari?"

"As you know, my father, Rashid Ben Ari, is semi-retired," Kumar said. "He has turned a great deal of the business of running the country over to me. There are many changes I want to make, but I have discovered I cannot make them by myself. I need help, if I am to bring Abdu Resaba into the twenty-first century."

Ron Marshall steepled his bony fingers and waited.

"Health is one of my main concerns," Kumar went on. "There's a hospital in the capital city of Bir Chagga, but the doctors as well as the nursing staff must be brought up-to-date on new techniques in medicine. I'd also like to open clinics in the smaller areas of the country, to educate people on health care and birth control."

As he spoke, Kumar warmed to his subject, for all that he said was true. There *was* need for change in Abdu Resaba.

It was also true, of course, that he lusted after Josie McCall. If he could, as the Americans said, kill two birds with one stone, all the better.

"To do all the things I want to do," he continued, "I need the assistance of someone from your organization who has an administrative as well as a medical background." He paused, and looking thoughtful, continued. "Of course I wouldn't expect International Health to bear the expenses for such an endeavor. It isn't money that we lack, you see. It's technical know-how. Naturally I would make a donation to the organization."

Ron Marshall leaned forward in his chair.

"I thought perhaps a small donation of..." Kumar paused to take another cigarette out of the gold case and tap it gently on the desk. Before he could light it, Ron Marshall leapt up and flicked the lighter he'd quickly pulled from his breast pocket.

Kumar breathed in the smoke, murmured his thanks, and said, "Three million dollars? To begin with, I mean."

"Three..." Ron Marshall's Adam's apple did a yo-yo-like bounce. "We...we'll do anything we can to help, Prince Ben Ari. I know just the man to set things up for you."

"Actually, Mr. Marshall, I already have someone in mind. A young woman who works for you in Guatemala, a Miss McCall. I've met her and I must say I'm quite impressed with her background, and also by the fact that she's had some experience in the Middle East. She's the person I'd like to see come to Abdu Resaba."

"Well I...I don't know how Miss McCall would feel about that." Marshall ran a finger around his stiff white collar. "You see, she's up for a promotion, and we had almost decided to send her to our main European office in Paris."

Kumar's dark eyebrows came together in a frown, but before he could speak, Marshall said, "But I can assure you that the man I first thought of is an excellent administrator. I'm sure that he—"

"I don't think so." Kumar started to rise. "If Miss McCall is unable to take the assignment I'll give up on the idea, at least for a year or two."

"Oh, no! I...we wouldn't want you to do that. I mean, we want to...to be of whatever assistance we can." Marshall cleared his throat. "I'll speak to Miss McCall. I don't know how she'll feel about accepting the assignment, but I'll do my best to convince her."

"I hope so," Kumar said. "If you don't..." He let the words hang and watched with fascination as Marshall's Adam's apple yo-yoed at the thought of losing the three million dollars that until a few moments before had been almost in his grasp.

"I'd like you to talk to Miss McCall as soon as you can." Kumar eased himself back into the chair. "I'll have my bank wire the three million—" Kumar studied the end of his cigarette "—just as soon as Miss McCall arrives in Abdu Resaba."

Ron Marshall dabbed at his upper lip with a clean white handkerchief. "I'll call her," he said. "I'll order her to Washington immediately."

"Ask," Kumar said in a deceptively soft voice. "Do not order." He stood, dismissing Ron Marshall. "I'd appreciate your speaking to her as soon as possible," he said. "Today, if it won't inconvenience you."

"No, of course not. Today. Yes indeed, today," Marshall said, as he backed himself out of the door.

"Well, well, well." James T. Harwood leaned back in his chair and grinned at Kumar. "Three million dollars? Miss McCall must be quite a woman."

"She is," Kumar said with a satisfied smile. "Believe me, James, she really is."

Two days after Kumar's return to Abdu Resaba, Josie arrived in Washington. Ron Marshall had refused to tell her over the phone why he had summoned her, but she knew what it was. At last, just as she had hoped, the assignment had come through. She was going to Paris. And while she would be sorry to leave Guatemala, Paris was the answer to all that she had worked so hard for.

Marshall rose from the big leather chair behind his desk. "Hello!" he said in a too hearty voice and held out his hand to her.

Josie shook it. It was so unpleasantly damp that it took every bit of her willpower not to wipe her own hand on the skirt of her tailored dress.

He seemed nervous. She wondered why. Offering a smile, she said, "Well, here I am. I hope I've come all this way to hear some good news."

"Good news?" He cleared his throat and motioned her to the chair opposite him. "Well...yes, I hope you'll think so."

Josie clasped her hands together. "I've been waiting and hoping for this," she said. "I've never been to Paris and—"

"Not Paris," he said interrupting her. "No, no, I'm afraid it isn't Paris. Actually it's something quite different and very...uh, challenging. Actually quite exotic."

"Exotic?" Her smile faded, she looked puzzled. "I'm not going to Paris?"

"Well, no." He cleared his throat. "Actually, Miss McCall, you've been assigned to Abdu Resaba for a year."

Josie's green eyes widened as the words "Abdu Resaba" slowly sank in. In a voice of barely suppressed rage, she asked, "What did you say?"

Marshall reclined farther back in his chair. "Abdu... Abdu Resaba. It's a small oil-rich country in the Middle East. It borders on—"

"I know what it borders on." Josie stood, and with both hands flat on the desk, glared at Ron Marshall. "But if you think I'm going there, you've got another think coming."

He blanched, swallowed, and said, "Now, now, now," in a voice which was intended to be soothing but was, in reality, a wheedling whine.

"Don't now me!" She was angrier than she had ever been in her life, because she knew that somehow, some way, Kumar Ben Ari had arranged this.

She wouldn't go. That was it. Final. No discussion. She'd stay in Guatemala forever if she had to, but she would not, by God, go to Abdu Resaba.

Chin high, mouth firm, she said, "I won't go."

"But you... you have no choice," he sputtered.

"I'll return to Guatemala."

"I'm afraid that's impossible."

"What do you mean impossible?"

"I've already assigned someone else. Alicia Mendoza. She'd asked to be sent somewhere in Central America. She's Mexican and her Spanish is excellent."

"So's mine."

Marshall shook his head. "It's been decided."

Josie balled her hands into fists and held them to her sides so that she wouldn't leap across the desk and throttle Ron Marshall.

"Prince Kumar Ben Ari is making a three-million-dollar donation to International Health," he said. "If you don't go, I'm afraid I'll have to accept your resignation. The prince is a powerful friend of the United States, a friend we most desperately need in that part of the world. To refuse his request for aid—aid he is quite willing to pay for—would not be a good diplomatic move."

He leaned across the desk. "Surely you're aware of how desperately we are in need of money, Miss McCall. Three million dollars will feed a lot of hungry people."

Yes, it would feed a lot of hungry people. But Kumar wasn't just buying aid for his country, he was trying to buy her! She'd been right about him, he *was* a chauvinist, determined to get his own way no matter what the cost.

"Your office will be in the U.S. consulate building in Abdu Resaba," Ron Marshall said. "You'll be under their protection." He clasped his hands together as if in prayer. "It's only for a year," he said. "After that, I promise you Paris." He looked at her pleadingly. "Please, think about it, Miss McCall. Think what we can do with the money. There's the crisis in Bosnia, Somalia, Ethiopia..."

He let the names dangle before her, and she knew it was true. So many countries, so many people in crisis. Hundreds of thousands who would starve without the help of organizations like International Health.

"Prince Kumar specifically asked for me?"

Marshall nodded. "He said he'd met you and that he had been impressed."

"I see."

"Since his father's semiretirement, he's the acting head of one of the richest oil-producing countries in the world. How could I say no?"

"How, indeed?" she said sarcastically.

"It's only for a year." There was a whine in his voice, a basset hound droop to his eyes.

A year. Josie looked down at the hands clasped tightly around her purse. She thought what it would be like there in that desert country, where Kumar Ben Ari was the total, the complete authority. And felt a sudden chill of dread run, like an icy finger, down her spine.

She tried to shake the feeling off. She was a United States citizen. Even in Abdu Resaba she would be under the protection of the United States consulate. There was nothing to be afraid of.

But when she left the office and went back down the corridor to the elevator, she remembered the desire—and yes, the anger—in Kumar Ben Ari's eyes the last time she had seen him.

This time she could not push away the fear.

Josie flew back to Guatemala the following afternoon and arrived to find that Alicia Mendoza had already taken over her office. She bit back her anger and tried to be civil because this wasn't Mendoza's fault. She explained the files and brought the other woman up on the work that had been done and the work that still needed doing. She took her on a tour of the clinics and introduced her to the different staffs.

The hard part came when she said goodbye to all the people she had grown to love during the years she had been in Guatemala. There were nurses she had trained, doctors she had worked with. All such good people, such good friends.

With all her heart she had wanted to tell Ron Marshall to go to hell. But she couldn't do that. She had worked too hard and long to get where she was. She had no choice, she had to go to Abdu Resaba.

But as she threw clothes into suitcases and packed boxes of things she wanted to take with her, her anger flamed until it was like a hard, unswallowable knot in her throat. She hated Kumar Ben Ari for forcing her to come to his country. She would go and she would do the job she had been assigned to do. But she would stay as far away from Kumar as she could, and if he even so much as laid a pinkie on her she'd run screaming to the embassy. He might have won the battle, but he hadn't won the war.

The flight from Mexico City to Paris had been uneventful. When she came off the jetway with the other passengers, a well-dressed man approached her.

"Miss McCall?" he asked. "Miss Josephine McCall?"

Josie nodded.

"I am Nawab al-Haj. Prince Kumar Ben Ari has asked me to meet you and to escort you to Abdu Resaba." He reached for her carryon bag. "The prince's private plane is waiting. I have sent another man to collect your luggage. If you will come with me, please."

"But I have a connecting flight to Cairo, then to Abdu Resaba."

"The prince thought you would be more comfortable on his private jet." Al-Haj took her arm. "This way," he said.

She looked around, as though appealing to the other passengers for help, then with a resigned shrug let Kumar's man lead her through the terminal.

They passed through corridor after corridor, until at last they came to a door that opened onto a runway. She saw a plane that was surely as large as the one she had flown to Paris on. The purple-and-white colors of Abdu Resaba were emblazoned on the side, along with the words, "His Imperial Majesty."

"I'm sure you'll find the aircraft quite comfortable," al-Haj said. "You have had a long flight, yes? So perhaps after lunch you would enjoy a bath and a bit of rest."

A bath? On a plane? Ali Baba time, she thought, and gave herself a mental shake. This was all happening too fast, she needed time to catch up.

But there was no time. Kumar's man took her arm and led her up the steps to the entrance of the plane, where two robed women waited.

"Greetings, *madame,*" one of them said. "Your baggage has already arrived, so when you are settled we will be ready for takeoff. Please to follow me, yes?"

Josie looked from Nawab al-Haj to the young woman, then with a lift of her shoulders followed her into a salon the size of a comfortable living room. The soft leather sofa was a golden beige color. There were leather armchairs, a round table with a bouquet of red roses and a box of Swiss chocolates. There were magazines, soft lighting and a movie screen.

Josie took one of the chairs. The young woman asked her to fasten her seat belt.

"How long is the flight to Abdu Resaba?" Josie asked.

"Seven hours, *madame*," the young woman said. "But you will sleep so that when you arrive you will feel rested." She offered a hesitant smile. "I am Melea. The other attendant is Fatima. If there is anything you desire, you have only to ask."

The engines revved and a voice speaking in a language Josie did not understand came over the loudspeaker.

"We are ready for takeoff," Melea said. "Please do not be nervous, *madame*. Abdel is a most good pilot."

Josie closed her eyes and clutched the arms of the chair. "I'm not nervous," she said between clenched teeth.

The plane raced across the runway, and with a final burst of speed, lifted into the air. Still Josie kept her eyes closed and did not open them until Melea asked, "May I bring you a glass of champagne, *madame?*"

"Yes, that would be nice," she said, forgetting for a moment that it was champagne that had gotten her into this situation in the first place.

A half hour into the air, lunch was served. Hearts of palm vinaigrette was followed by a tender chateaubriand, fresh asparagus, and finally strawberry crepes that melted in Josie's mouth. Instead of coffee she had a second glass of champagne, and by the time she finished she was so relaxed she could barely keep her eyes open.

"Your bath is ready," Fatima said while Melea cleared the table. "If you will follow me, *madame*."

The bathroom, while small, was luxurious. A black marble tub, recessed into the tile-covered floor, looked as if it were big enough for two. Had Kumar ever bathed here? Josie wondered. And with whom?

Fatima took a vial of oil from the selection near the tub and removed the stopper. "This is your scent is it not, *madame?*" she asked.

Josie looked at her, surprised, and said, "Yes, but how did you...?" But she knew. Kumar had recognized the perfume she had worn in California. He'd had it purchased and put on his plane for her use.

It was as if he had been spying on her, learning her secrets, and that frightened her. What else did he know about her? And how in the world could she cope with the kind of money and power he had, once she was on his turf?

These were the thoughts that troubled her as she watched Fatima pour a splash of perfumed oil into the hot water. When she had, Fatima indicated a pale green silk robe on the chest near the door, and said, "This is for you. When you have finished your bath, I will show you to the bedroom."

Josie lay back in the water scented with her perfume and looked at the pale green robe laid out on the chest. Nile green to match her eyes?

In spite of the warmth of the water, she shivered. Kumar had arranged all of this; the transfer to Abdu Resaba, his private jet, her special perfume and a silk robe that matched her eyes. What else did he have planned?

She felt overwhelmed with a sense of unreality, for it was as if she had sleepwalked into another world. Kumar's world.

She slid up to her chin in the frothy water, confused by the thoughts skittering round in her brain. Why me? she wondered. Why of all the women Kumar Ben Ari knew, and she'd bet her last dollar he knew thousands, had he gone to the trouble of forcing her to come to his country?

Was it because of her animosity toward Middle Eastern men? Had she, because of her frankness, angered
him so much that he had gone to all this trouble to get
her—she swallowed hard—exactly where he wanted her?

It was a scary thought. She would be thousands of
miles from home, out of her element, in a country ruled
by a man who still believed that women had to be robed
and veiled and hidden behind tall stone walls.

Well, by damn, *she* wouldn't be ruled. No matter what
Ron Marshall had said, if Kumar Ben Ari thought she
was going to kowtow to him he had another think coming. She was an American woman; she didn't kowtow to
anybody.

When finally she had bathed and dried herself, Josie
put on the green silk robe and left the bathroom. Fatima was waiting outside the door, and with a "Follow
me, please," led Josie down the corridor to the bedroom.

The white sheets—silk, of course—had been turned
back. The curtains had been drawn, the bedside lamp
lighted.

"If there is anything you wish, you have only to ring
the bell above your head," Fatima said. "We are here to
serve you. Please do not hesitate to call upon us."

Like a silent shadow she went out and closed the door.

Leaving Josie alone in this strange bed, as the plane
sped on toward Abdu Resaba.

Chapter 5

Below lay the stretch of endless desert dunes, rising and falling like a moonscape that seemed not a part of this planet. There was no sign of a village, a house or a highway, nothing to break the miles of sand turned golden in the early morning light.

The plane began its descent and the mountains came into view, severe and granite hard, without a tree, a bush or a touch of green to relieve the sawtooth harshness.

This was Kumar Ben Ari's land, and as Josie peered out of the window she felt a sense of foreboding. And anger. She had expected Paris, and if it had not been for Kumar she might now have been flying over that most beautiful of cities, gazing down at Notre Dame, the Eiffel Tower and the Seine instead of this dreadful loneliness of mountain and desert.

She was here because Kumar had pulled official strings; he had forced her to come, and she would never forgive him for that. Now that she was here, she would do the job she had been sent to do. God knows there had been other assignments she hadn't particularly liked, but she had always stuck it out, as she would here in Abdu Resaba. When her year was up, she would be on the first plane out.

As for Kumar, she would have as little to do with him as possible.

As the plane came lower, the walled city of Bir Chagga came into view and she saw white buildings with moorish domes and arches gleaming white in the morning sun. The plane dipped sideways and there on a hill overlooking the city she saw the palace, surely as large as England's Windsor Castle, but far more beautiful. The walls were the color of rich, thick cream. The sun sparkled on turrets of gleaming mosaic and cylindrical towers in shades of heavenly blue. On the very top of the highest tower flew the purple-and-white flag of Abdu Resaba.

This was Kumar Ben Ari's home, his father's kingdom. It didn't matter what diplomatic means he had used to get her here, he had commanded and she had come.

Ron Marshall had said her office would be in the same building as the American consulate. If there was a problem, if Kumar dared step over the line of diplomatic propriety, she'd be on the first plane out. He might have coerced her into accepting an assignment she didn't want, but she was an American citizen. He could not force her to stay against her will.

On the final approach she checked herself out in the full-length bedroom mirror. The tailored suit in an ivory-oatmeal shade was smart and expensive. With it she wore white pumps and a matching bag. Her hair was combed back off her face into a chignon. She looked smart and professional, and that's how she would behave from now on.

The plane circled lower. Melea came to the bedroom door and said, "Please to come to the salon, *madame*. We will be landing in a few moments."

"Thank you, Melea." During the flight the young woman had worn a white robe, but she had not been veiled. Now, however, she had changed to a dark robe and her face was covered from just below her eyes to her chin.

Josie stared for a moment before she looked away. More than anything, this sudden change in Melea brought home to Josie that she was indeed entering a land where men were the rulers and women had but to obey.

Melea took the seat across from her, and offering a smile, said, "It will be a smooth landing. Please do not worry."

Josie tried not to, but three feet off the narrow landing strip she clenched her teeth and closed her eyes. The plane touched down, sped like a silver arrow across the tarmac and finally slowed. Only then did Josie open her eyes, unfasten her seat belt and look out of the window. A long black stretch limo with the purple-and-white Abdu Resaba flag waited next to the plane.

While she watched, workers in dark robes and head coverings hurried to affix stairs to the now open door of the plane. Nawab al-Haj came out of the cockpit and motioned Josie forward. Melea and Fatima stepped aside to let her pass.

The hot air hit her like a physical blow. She gripped the railing, but before she could start down the stairs, Fatima said, "A moment, *madame*."

Two robed men quickly unrolled a red carpet from the bottom of the steps of the plane and laid it out so that it reached the rear door of the limo where a robed chauffeur stood at attention. When the carpet was in place the chauffeur opened the door and Prince Kumar Ben Ari stepped out into the sunlight.

Josie looked down at him. Shock took her breath as he strode purposefully forward. When they had met in California he had worn western clothes, tailored suits, a tuxedo and he had looked not unlike any of the other men who had attended Jenny's wedding.

He was different now. Attired in a white *djellaba*, with his dark hair covered by a *ghutra*, the typical Arabian male headdress, he looked foreign and mysterious, a man from a world she knew so little about. His skin seemed darker, his brows heavier, his eyes, when he gazed up at her, more sensuously threatening.

That very first day at the airport in Los Angeles she had thought him good-looking, but in Arabian clothes he was every woman's idea of a desert sheikh, devastatingly handsome, so outrageously masculine she wanted to duck back into the plane and run for cover.

He walked across the red carpet toward her. *"Marhaban,"* he said. "Welcome to my country."

Josie took a deep breath and started down the stairs. When she reached the bottom step, he held out his hand. She took it, nodded and said in as formal a voice as she could manage, "Good morning, Prince Ben Ari."

"Good morning," he responded in an equally formal voice. "I hope the trip was not too tiring."

"Not at all. I was quite comfortable, thank you."

"I'm glad." He took her arm. "Please, let me escort you to my car."

Car? It looked half as long as the *Queen Mary*.

The chauffeur bowed and opened the door. She slipped inside. The air was cool, the leather seats as soft as silk. Kumar came in beside her. He said something she didn't understand to the chauffeur, and with a soft purr of the engine the limo started.

"I'm so pleased you decided to come to Abdu Resaba," Kumar said.

Josie turned her cool green gaze in his direction. "I had no choice," she said stiffly. "I'm here because I was ordered to come. If I hadn't, I would have lost my job. I couldn't afford to do that."

He looked at her as if to say something, then frowned and turned away. A few days ago when he'd received word that Josie was coming to Abdu Resaba he had felt a sense of triumph. Now, he felt only shame. That bothered him more than he had thought it would. Never before had he forced a woman to do anything she didn't want to do. Women had always come to him willingly, eagerly. For all his life he'd had but to beckon to a woman who struck his fancy, whether a dancing girl or a lady of the French aristocracy.

Josie McCall was different. She was the only woman who had ever looked at him with something very like disdain. Even worse, she had judged him without knowing him. She had stepped on his male ego and he had been determined to bring her to Abdu Resaba to prove...what? That he had the power to do it?

He'd never done anything like this before. Why had he now? Why with this particular woman?

He shot her a sideways glance. She sat regally beside him, looking straight ahead. Her face in profile was classically beautiful. The pale skin was smooth and soft as the underbelly of a nightingale. She had high cheekbones and a patrician nose, and lips so sweetly curved it was all he could do, even now with that look of severity, not to sweep her into his arms and press his mouth to hers.

He remembered, with a tightening of his body, how those lips had softened under his the night of Mike and Jenny's dress rehearsal, how for that brief instant her body had heated and swayed to his.

That was why he had brought her here; that was why he would keep her until she surrendered to him. When he'd had his fill of her, he would let her go.

It was true, of course, that he wanted to improve the medical facilities in Abdu Resaba. But it was also true that anyone on the staff of the International Health Organization could have done the job. He hadn't wanted anyone else; he had only wanted Josie McCall.

He began to tell her about the buildings they were passing. "The Ministry of Foreign Affairs," he said, indicating a thirty-story building of polished stone and glass. "The Abdu Resaba National Bank, the National Assembly Building, the Great Mosque, the Abdu Resaba Oil Company."

The buildings looked modern, clean and cool in the early morning heat. The boulevard was lined with stately royal palms. There were parks with fountains of water sparkling in the sun, and the street was filled with robed men and veiled women.

"We're entering the Diplomatic Quarter now," Kumar explained. "The building on the right is the French embassy. The Italian and the Spanish embassies are next. Across the street is the Saudi embassy, the Libyan and the Nigerian consulates. On the next street are most of the South American consulates."

When they turned the corner and Josie saw a two-story building surrounded by a tall iron fence, Kumar said, "That is the building of the Unites States consulate. Your office is in the right wing. Mr. Aubrey Bonner is the consul in charge. Edward Petersen is his assistant. Their residences are right next door."

"And mine?" Josie asked.

"Yours is not. I have arranged a house for you on another street. That is where we're going now."

Josie looked at him, surprised and disturbed because she would much rather have had a place next to the consul and his assistant, where she would have felt some measure of protection.

Before she could offer an objection the limousine turned into a palm-lined driveway and there, beyond high hedges, a tall iron fence and a gate, she saw the house. It was one story, of pure white stone, with gleaming mosaic arches and a blue door.

A uniformed guard saluted as the limo passed through the gate, and when they reached the house a robed woman, followed by two other women and a man, hurried out.

The limo stopped and the chauffeur hurried around to open Josie's door, then Kumar's. The four people in front of the house bowed.

"This is your secretary," Kumar said to Josie, indicating a short, rather stout woman. "Sarida Barakat."

The woman bobbed her head.

In her mid-thirties, with a hawklike nose and bushy black eyebrows, she was not an attractive woman—until she smiled. When she did, her eyes warmed and welcomed. She wore a dark brown robe and her hair was covered by a brown cloth.

"How do you do? I'm afraid I don't speak your language very well yet," Josie said.

"I speak the English, *madame*. I studied at the University of Beirut before all of the trouble in that city, and I have worked for the American-Abdu Resaba Oil Company here. I hope I may be of service to you."

"I'm sure you will be, Miss Barakat. I'll be grateful for your help."

"And these are your servants," Kumar said. "Zohra and Karmah."

They bobbed their heads and smiled.

Kumar motioned the man forward. "This is Saoud," he said.

The man was almost seven feet tall. Josie guessed his age to be somewhere between fifty and sixty. His skin was like fine black parchment. He wore a dark gold robe of a heavy material and his head was covered by a clean white cloth. His eyes were kind, his smile was gentle. He was barefoot.

He took a step forward, bowed from the waist, and murmured, *"Marhaban."*

"Thank you," Josie responded, and offered her hand. His fingers were long and bony, his grip was firm. When he let her go he stepped back, said something to Kumar, then hurried to the car to get her luggage.

"Come." Kumar took her arm. "Let me show you your house. The women will unpack and prepare your bath when you're ready. A meal has been prepared, in case you would like something to eat before you rest. If it's not to your liking you have only to tell Zohra what you would prefer instead, and she will fix it."

He exerted a small pressure on her arm and she let him lead her into the house, if indeed house was the proper name for it. The columned arches they passed through were intricately carved. The entranceway was mosaic tiled in geometric designs in shades of blue and gray and pale pink.

Kumar motioned her to proceed him into a small patio. Here there were orange and lemon trees heavy with fruit, and a white marble fountain that bubbled water colored the same pale pink shade of the tiles.

Beyond the patio was the living room. Most of the tile floor was covered by an oriental rug in colors of deep red and gold. There were two seven-foot sofas, low easy chairs and tasseled floor pillows. Curtains that looked as if they had been woven from threads of gold hung at the windows. Bright and colorful glass lamps were placed on carved tables.

Kumar turned one of them on. "Blessed is He who made constellations in the skies and placed therein a lamp and a moon giving light." He smiled. "That is from the Koran," he said. "I'm sorry that I cannot give you the moon, I can only offer light."

Josie felt a blush of color flood her cheeks, and though she had been strangely moved by his words, made herself say in as cool a voice as she could manage, "It's a lovely room. And the house is very nice."

"But you have not yet seen the rest of it. Please allow me to show you a few of the other rooms."

He led her through marble pillars into an alcove off the living room. It was small and dimly lighted by a lantern of deep blue glass that hung from the filigree gold ceiling. The three walls were of even more intricately carved filigree work.

Beneath the back wall was a wide blue velvet sofa and silk pillows in a softer shade of blue. A musical instrument that looked somewhat like a mandolin rested at one end of the sofa. One small table, inlaid with ivory, held a golden incense jar. Another held a single gold candlestick.

It was a warmly intimate room, beautifully, strangely seductive, and Josie wondered as she stood in the entrance if lovers had ever made love on that wide blue sofa. With the thought her cheeks flushed and she backed away.

She followed Kumar through long, cool corridors to the dining room and into a smaller salon that was, he said, for afternoon tea. In the library there were floor-to-ceiling bookcases filled with books in Arabian, Spanish and French, as well as books in English in both fiction and nonfiction that she had seen a week ago on the *New York Times* bestseller list.

He stood back as a smile softened her features, pleased that she was pleased. For though he had forced her to come to his country, he wanted her to have every comfort he could provide.

The house had been pleasant to begin with, but during the past two weeks he'd had it redecorated. He'd flown in an interior designer from Paris and had brought in an artisan who had recently redesigned several rooms in the palace, to oversee all the work and the men and women who toiled from dawn to midnight to complete the job before Josie's arrival.

He led Josie through another patio to another corridor. "Your bedroom," he said, indicating the closed doors. Then he opened them and motioned for her to enter.

The room was a shimmering symphony of white-and-gold. The round bed in the middle of a raised dais was canopied in delicate handmade lace. The furniture was white, trimmed in gold, and on one of the dressers there was a bouquet of white roses.

He indicated the mirrored closet that occupied the length of one wall. "I've taken the liberty of adding some things to your wardrobe," he said. "Robes that I thought you might enjoy wearing."

Before she could respond he drew back one of the gossamer curtains and indicated a terraced garden. There were flowers everywhere, wide green ferns, blossoming trees and a swimming pool.

"This is your private garden and pool," he said. "No one will bother you here." The barest suggestion of a smile crooked his mouth. "Unless, of course, you wish to be bothered."

When she offered no answering smile, he let the curtain drop back into place. "You're angry with me for bringing you here," he said. "I'm sorry that you are."

"Why did you?"

"I wanted to bring my country's medical facilities up-to-date. There are many problems in Abdu Resaba. The hospital must be modernized. I want to build more clinics, educate more people in health care, birth control and proper diet. You've done this is other countries. I knew you could help me."

"So could a lot of other people in our organization."

"I didn't want other people." He gazed at her until the silence became like the stillness in that final moment just before the winds of a hurricane hit.

"Let me go," she said, although he had not moved to touch her.

He shook his head. "I cannot," he said softly.

"Prince Kumar—"

"Kumar. Only Kumar."

"You shouldn't have brought me here against my will," she said. "You had no right." She lifted her chin and her green eyes were cold and angry.

He stepped back a pace. "Nevertheless, you are here," he said. And now there was no gentleness in his voice. "There is a reception at the palace tomorrow night for the United States consul and his assistant, also for the members of my cabinet and their wives. I will send my car for you at seven."

She wanted to refuse, but before she could speak he said, "It's an official reception for your consul. I will expect you to be there."

Her mouth tightened. "Very well."

"Until tomorrow night, then." And when she didn't answer, he said, "If there is anything you desire, you have only to ask one of the servants. They are here to serve you."

He took her hand and she felt the touch of his lips against her skin before he turned away.

The robe did not disguise the broadness of his shoulders as he strode from the room. She rubbed her thumb across the hand he had kissed, and when she felt the slight dampness from his lips, a quiver ran through her. He had brought her here against her will and she hated him for that. He had no right to do what he had done, to use his power to make her do something she didn't want to do.

And yes, she hated him because when he touched her she felt the same hot curl of flame lick at her insides. It was an attraction she could not deny, an attraction she would fight with everything that was in her.

With a shake of her head she went into the bathroom to bathe.

The scent of her own special perfume filled the room. The woman Zohra turned toward her. "Yes?" she said. "You like?" She pointed to the dozen or so other oils on a shelf near the tub. "If no, we change. Yes?"

"Yes," Josie said. "I mean no. This is fine."

Zohra pointed to Josie. "I undress you now."

"No," Josie said firmly. "I undress myself."

The other woman shook her head. "Prince Ben Ari say it is my job to do everything for you. I draw bath. I dress, undress. Master tell me—"

"*Your* master, not mine. Thank you, Zohra. You may leave now."

Zohra hung her head and pointed a finger at her own chest. "You do not like me?" she asked.

"I like you very much, but I will bathe myself." Josie pointed at the door. "Until later."

Zohra went, and when the door closed behind her, Josie stripped out of her clothes and stepped into the steaming musky water. Sheer luxury, she thought, as she had on the plane, took some getting used to. If this was to be her home for a year, she might as well enjoy it.

Tomorrow night she would go to the palace, because it was a matter of diplomatic protocol to attend a dinner at which the consul of the United States was to be the honored guest. And yes, because she was dying to see it. But other than occasions where her presence was demanded, she would stay as far away from Prince Kumar as she could. She had absolutely no intention of letting him anywhere near her again.

She lifted the hand he had kissed from the soapy water and blew the suds away. Then, she did not know why, she kissed the skin his lips had kissed. "Kumar," she whispered, and slipping farther down into the scented water, she closed her eyes.

She was even more beautiful than he remembered. And just as cool and remote as she had been in California. But she was here; that's what was important. At last he had Miss Josie McCall right where he wanted her. In *his* land, *his* domain.

It was only a matter of time. He would go slowly. He would neither push nor insist. He would be patient, because he knew that in the end his patience and persistence would be rewarded. It always had been.

Josie McCall was no different than any other woman. More of a challenge perhaps, but he liked a challenge. It made the waiting exciting, the final result more enjoyable.

Kumar leaned back against the fine leather seat of the limousine and smiled. She was a delectable woman from the top of her sunlit hair all the way down to her toes, and he had every intention of sampling all of that delectability.

Sooner or later.

He closed his eyes and felt his body grow hard with need, a need he knew could be eased by any of the dancing girls at the Palais Royale. But it wasn't dancing girls he wanted, it was Miss Josie McCall. And by Allah, he was determined to have her.

He shifted to try to ease the pain in his groin, and decided that it would have to be sooner rather than later.

Chapter 6

Josie debated at length about how to dress. This would be the first time she would meet the consul and his assistant, as well as the members of Prince Kumar's cabinet and their wives. A good first impression was important. At last, because she knew it was the custom in this part of the world for a woman not to bare her shoulders, her arms or her legs, she chose an ivory silk georgette blouse with a Venetian lace collar and cuffs, and silky, soft ivory pleated pants, so full they gave the appearance of a skirt.

With the outfit she wore a gold chain belt, a wide gold bracelet with matching earrings, and high-heeled gold sandals. She swept her hair back in the usual chignon, applied very little makeup and a dab of perfume behind her ears and on her wrists.

A white stretch limousine arrived promptly at seven. The chauffeur opened the door, but before she could enter, Saoud, moving silently as a ghost on his bare feet, appeared at her side.

"Allow me, *madame*," he said, and taking Josie's arm helped her into the car before he got into the front seat beside the chauffeur.

He sat very straight for one so tall, and it seemed to Josie, observing him from the back seat, that he was tense, alert. He turned his head whenever a car passed, and when suddenly a black Ferrari cut alongside, Josie saw him dart a look at the other car and with a muttered curse he reached inside his robe.

He put a cautioning hand on the driver's arm. The limo slowed and fell back. The black Ferrari moved ahead of them and in front of them and slowed down so that the two vehicles were only a few feet apart.

Saoud whispered something to the chauffeur and the limo leapt forward at a speed that threw Josie back against the cushioned seat.

"What is it?" she asked, alarmed.

"It is nothing to concern yourself with, *madame*." He flipped the mirrored visor down. "I assure you, there is no need for alarm."

But why had he dropped back, then sped ahead? They were in an official car with the standard of Abdu Resaba painted discreetly on the side. Surely no one would bother a vehicle that belonged to the royal family. Or would they? Was there trouble here she didn't know about?

Before she could ask, Saoud said, "We will be at the palace in another few minutes. You see? There it is, on the rise of the hill."

Whatever alarm Josie might have felt vanished at the sight. The road leading up to the palace was lined on both sides with royal palms and lights that glowed to guide their way. The palace, too, was aglow with light, and for a moment she felt as though she had awakened in the midst of a wonderful fairy tale, that the white limo wasn't a limo at all but a magic carpet taking her up a sweeping road that led to a castle right out of the *Arabian Nights*.

And to the prince who waited there.

She felt a flare of excitement and tried to push it away. She was here because she had been forced to come by a man in whom she had no interest. This was all very glamorous; the private plane, the house he had arranged for her, the Arabian palace they were approaching. But... and the *but* was a very big one, she had not come to Abdu Resaba of her own free will. As long as she was here as an American representative of International Health, she would be forced by protocol to be polite. But that's all. She would offer nothing beyond that.

They drove closer to an archway that curved over the road. The chauffeur blinked his lights and two armed guards, wearing long red robes and fezes, stepped forward, weapons that looked like Uzi machine guns at the ready.

"*Baraka,* stop!" one of them called out.

The other shone a flashlight inside the car.

"The lady is a guest of Prince Kumar Ben Ari from the United States of America," Saoud said.

"Ah." One of the guards nodded. "It is you, Saoud. *Salam Alekom.*"

"And upon you peace," the black man answered. "May we go on?"

The guard nodded. And to Josie he said in English, "Have an enjoyable evening, *madame.*"

As they proceeded up the hill, the palace seemed to grow in proportion, rising in cream-colored magnificence, its turrets and towers pointed skyward in the shadow of the moon. As they drew closer she saw there were terraced lawns, gardens and lighted fountains that rose like prisms of clear crystal in the evening air.

The curved portal entrance rose to a height of one hundred feet. Mosaic tile in shades of gold and blue and lavender were inlaid upon the color of cream, richly beautiful even in the shade of night.

Saoud opened her door, and helping her out of the limousine, offered his arm to escort her toward the entrance where a man and woman waited beneath the arches.

The man came forward. "*Mesa al khair,* evening of goodness," he said by way of greeting.

"*Mesa annour,*" Josie responded.

"You speak our language," the veiled women said.

"I speak a little," Josie acknowledged.

"Welcome to the royal house of Ben Ari. You will to follow me, please."

"Go with them." Saoud bowed from his waist. "Have a pleasant evening, *madame.*"

"Thank you, Saoud." She hesitated for a moment, then turned to follow the man and woman through the arched portal into the palace.

Her first impression, in addition to the grandeur that took her breath, was of clean coolness and a sense of peace. She stopped for a moment, gazing about her in wonder. The walls and ceiling of the first room were in brilliant colors of mosaic tiles such as she had seen at the Alhambra in Granada and the Alcazar in Seville. Marble columns rose in beautiful simplicity to the curved, intricately carved arches.

The man faded away into a darkened corridor, but the woman motioned Josie to follow her through a patio perfumed with jasmine and orange blossom, down another wide corridor and finally to a tall door where two robed men stood at attention. The woman spoke and one of the men sprang forward to open the door.

Josie stepped into a room that literally took away her breath. Two of the walls were done in green-and-gold mosaic, as was the three-story-high ceiling. One wall was draped in scarlet velvet, the other with a magnificent tapestry. Before she could recover another man hurried forward, bowed and asked, "Miss Josephine McCall?"

Josie nodded. In the room beyond she saw a group of people gathered around a central fountain. Kumar stood in the center of the group. He was speaking to someone, but when he saw her he murmured to the man at his side and hurried toward her.

He wore a robe of a deep red color threaded with gold. His head was uncovered and in the glow of the overhead lights his thick black hair glistened like the wings of a hawk.

"*Salam alekom,*" he said. "Welcome to my house."

"*Shukran,*" she answered.

"I didn't know you spoke our language."

"I speak a little, not very well I'm afraid."

Kumar smiled. "I will teach you all you need to know." And before Josie could respond, he offered his arm and led her to the group gathered near the fountain.

"This is Miss McCall," he said by way of a general introduction, and led her to a tall, spare man in his middle fifties.

"May I present your United States consul, Mr. Aubrey Bonner," Kumar said.

Bonner took her hand. "Miss McCall. How nice it is to meet you. I was delighted when I heard that International Health was sending someone to Abdu Resaba. If there is any way in which I can be of assistance, you need only ask. I understand your office will be in the consulate building and I look forward to seeing you there."

He turned to the man and woman standing next to him. "Please allow me to introduce my assistant, Ed Petersen, and his wife. Ed, Edith, this is Miss McCall."

Mr. Petersen was a wiry-looking man, so trim that she bet he ran three miles every morning before breakfast. He had a full head of gray hair and a trim mustache. His clothes were...Josie searched for the word and came up with "natty." His wife's weren't. Though her flowered dress was obviously expensive, it did little to improve her thirty-pounds-overweight figure.

Edith Petersen murmured a polite greeting, looked Josie up and down and said, "We must have tea some time soon."

Next Josie was introduced to the members of Kumar's cabinet and their wives. The men were polite and obviously curious. Their wives, both robed and veiled, were so shy they barely mumbled a greeting. But when Josie spoke a few words in their language they smiled and one of them, a young woman, began to speak to her. In a few moments so did the other women, all except Edith Petersen, who looked as though she disapproved of Josie's friendliness.

It was a little while before Josie noticed that the men had moved to one side of the room and the women to another. Although this annoyed her, she had been in both Guatemala and Mexico, as well as the Middle East long enough to know this was the custom and there was nothing she could do about it. Very likely the two sexes would come together over dinner, but in the meantime they would be separated. This would give her an opportunity to explain to the women why she had come to their country and perhaps even to elicit their help.

Before she could begin, however, Edith Petersen said in English, "I'm very glad to meet you, Miss McCall. It will be a blessing to have someone of my own kind to talk to. I have nothing in common with these women. They're light-years away from us intellectually."

Josie's face flushed with embarrassment, for herself and for the Abdu Resaba women. Barely controlling her outrage, she managed to say, "I agree that we're different, Mrs. Petersen, but I often think we have as much to learn from other ethnic groups as they have to learn from us."

With that she turned to the other women and said in her halting Arabic, "I have come to Abdu Resaba in the hope of helping to improve your medical facilities. Tomorrow I will visit your local hospital."

The young woman she had first spoken to shook her head. "Of course you mean to visit only the women's section of the hospital. It would not be proper to go into the wards where there are men."

"I'm a nurse." Josie smiled reassuringly. "I'm sure when I explain to the doctors and staff why I'm there, they will understand."

"I do not think so," another woman said. "Besides, the men are in one section of the hospital, where they are attended by the doctors and male nurses. The women's section is apart, attended by female nurses. If it is necessary for a doctor to see them, there is a woman doctor from Egypt who can be called upon in an emergency."

"Do you mean there isn't a staff doctor on hand, if a woman has a medical emergency?"

"No, there is not, *madame*," an older woman said. "It would be incorrect for a member of the opposite sex to look upon the body of a woman who is not his wife."

The other women nodded in agreement, while Josie stared at them and wondered how in the world she would break through hundreds of years of tradition to do the job she had come to do.

At dinner the men sat on floor cushions on one side of the low table, the women on the other.

Black olives, small tomatoes, pickled lemons, radishes, figs and dates were on the table when the soup was served. It was *harira*, a chicken soup that had been thickened with flour and eggs and flavored with pepper and cinnamon.

That was followed by artichokes in a lemon-and-saffron sauce, a sea bass covered with vegetables and spices presented on banana leaves, lamb cooked in a marinade and finally a steaming bowl of couscous.

It was not a meal to be hurried and almost two hours went by before the table was cleared and the wheat pudding and hot mint tea were served.

Like the other women, Josie had remained silent while the men did the talking. Now and then one of the men glanced at her. Several of them smiled and nodded, and a younger man whom she thought might be the husband of the young woman she had first spoken to passed her the bowl of figs and said in English, "You would like, yes?"

There was only one of them who looked at her differently than the others. He was a middle-aged man with a round, heavy jowled face and a salt-and-pepper mustache that curved down to meet a line of whiskers that circled his mouth. There was something about him, a sly, knowing, speculative look that made her uncomfortable, and when she saw him watching her she lowered her gaze.

Most of the conversation was far too fast for Josie to understand, but she sensed midway through the dinner that the discussion had become heated. The man with the speculative look said something in a loud voice, and when he did Aubrey Bonner's face got red. Before Bonner could say anything, Kumar spoke sharply to the man with the mustache. Not intimiated, Mr. Mustache growled something under his breath. The man next to him, a thin fellow with small eyes and a large nose added his two cents' worth, and suddenly all of the men at the table, including Aubrey Bonner and Edward Petersen, were shouting.

Kumar let it go on for perhaps two minutes before he struck the table with the flat of his hand, and in a voice so low Josie could barely hear said, "*Baraka!* Enough!"

In the silence that followed he turned to Aubrey Bonner and Ed Petersen. "I hope you will forgive the members of my cabinet for their bad manners," he said in English. "My great-grandfather had a way of dealing with such discourtesies, but alas times have changed and today it is frowned upon to cut out a man's tongue."

He turned to look at the man who had started it, and in a voice that sent a chill down Josie's spine he said, "Though there have been times when I have been tempted."

Without taking his gaze from the man, he dipped his fingers into the bowl of lemon water next to his plate and when he had wiped them on a clean napkin said, speaking so slowly and evenly that even Josie understood, "You have been discourteous to my guests, Sharif Kadiri. You owe them an apology."

Kadiri's mouth tightened. He did not speak.

"I'm waiting."

"Then wait!" Kadiri pushed himself back from the table. He snapped a string of words to the men on either side of him and all three of them stood and strode out of the room.

When they had gone there was silence. At last Kumar said, "Please accept my apologies, Mr. Bonner and Mr. Petersen. The behavior of my ministers was inexcusable."

"Not your fault," Bonner said. "But if I were you, Prince Kumar, I'd keep my eye on that fellow. He means to stir up trouble."

"I can assure you that it won't be anything I can't handle."

"There have been rumors—"

"That we should not discuss in front of the ladies." Kumar stood and offered a hand to Josie to bring her up beside him. "I'm sorry this had to happen the first time you have been in my home," he said. "I'll make sure it doesn't occur the next time you visit."

That ended the dinner party. The remaining members of Kumar's cabinet, embarrassed by what had happened, left with their wives. Aubrey Bonner asked if he could escort Josie back to her home, but before she could answer, Kumar said, "It's kind of you to offer, but I will escort Miss McCall."

He walked Bonner and the Petersens to the door and when he had bid them good-night he returned to Josie.

For a moment neither of them spoke. She was ill at ease and wished she hadn't let Aubrey Bonner leave without her. She didn't want to be here alone with Kumar.

"Would you care for an after-dinner drink?" he asked. "I didn't offer it before because of our customs, but we are alone now and we can have a brandy, if you'd like."

Without waiting for her answer, he went to a carved wall cabinet and took out a bottle of brandy. "I'm afraid the evening didn't turn out the way I planned," he said. "I'm sorry."

"Why was...? His name is Kadiri? Why was he so angry? Is it something political?"

"Matters of state," Kumar answered, and thought how like an American woman to want to discuss politics. An Arabian woman would never have asked such a question. But then, this woman wasn't like the women of his or any other Middle Eastern country.

A moment ago, when the others left, she had seemed anxious and ill at ease. Now she seemed more relaxed and strangely enough he found himself wanting to talk to her about his concerns and the things that worried him.

He took two crystal snifters from the cabinet and poured a splash of brandy into each of them before he motioned her to a low sofa under the tapestry and said, "Come and sit down for a moment and I will tell you what it is that troubles me."

He warmed his glass between his hands for a moment, then touched his glass to hers, and after he had taken a sip said, "There are men in my cabinet who want to sell our country's oil to Azrou Jadida instead of to the United States."

"Azrou Jadida?" Josie frowned. The country was small but powerful. It was bordered on one side by the Caspian Sea and on the other side by Il Efran. Last year they had invaded that country. Thousands of civilians had been killed, countless women had been raped. They had bombed and ravaged the land, and when they were finished they partitioned one third of Il Efran for themselves.

"It's a warlike country," she said with growing horror. "Surely you wouldn't consider selling oil to them."

"Of course not, but there are men in my cabinet who would, a faction led by Sharif Kadiri. He has gathered a group of supporters. There have been a few disturbances, but it isn't anything I can't handle."

"Is that why Saoud accompanied me to the palace tonight?"

"No, no, of course not." He avoided meeting her eyes and with a forced smile said, "You are a beautiful American woman. I had to make sure you were well protected."

Josie didn't return his smile. Instead she said, "On the way here a car moved up alongside of the limousine and cut in ahead of us. When it did, Saoud had the chauffeur drop back, then he sped up and passed the other car." She looked at him, her eyes level with his. "Are you in danger?" she asked. "Was the other car following us because they thought you might be inside?"

Kumar waited a moment before he answered. With a shake of his head he said, "You're imagining things, Josie. There are as many bad drivers here in Bir Chagga as there are in California. Undoubtedly the driver of the other car saw a limousine and wanted to race. I'm sure that's all it was."

"Why did you send Saoud with me?"

"He is my right hand," Kumar said, no longer smiling. "I trust him with my life, with all that I have, with all that I treasure. That is why I have placed him in your home. That is why he will accompany you wherever you go."

His eyes smoldered and darkened. She tried to look away, but she could not. It was as it had been that night in California. She wanted to say, as she had then, "Let me go." For he held her as surely as if he had tightened his hands around hers.

"It's late," she said. "I have to go."

A muscle in his cheek jumped, but his expression did not change. "Of course," he said, and getting to his feet he offered a hand to help her up.

When she stood beside him he did not let go of her hand, and they stood facing each other. It pleased him that she was tall, that in her high heels she stood eye to eye with him. He liked that. He remembered how it had been when they danced, how her body had fit so perfectly to his. He thought how it would be when they made love, for he knew in his heart that no matter how hard she tried to deny the attraction between them, the day would come when she would lie naked beside him.

He let go of her hand. "Come," he said, "I will take you home."

They went out through the now silent corridors and the patio scented with jasmine and orange blossoms. He spoke to a servant, and by the time they reached the entrance, a black convertible was waiting for them.

Saoud stood beside it. "You asked for the convertible," he said. "But it is best you take the limousine."

"Tonight I prefer the open car."

"It is dangerous."

"No, it is not."

"I will drive."

Kumar shook his head. "Not tonight, my friend."

"You will be vulnerable in an open car."

"It's late. There will be no danger." Kumar reached up to rest a hand on the tall man's shoulder. "Do as I say. And do not worry."

He turned away and opened the door for Josie. When he had helped her in, he went around to the driver's side.

The motor hummed to life and he started out of the circular driveway, down past the long rows of royal palms and the guardhouse, out finally to the highway.

"You don't mind the wind?" he asked.

She leaned her head back against the seat. "No, I like it."

"It would be better if your hair were loose. I'd like to see it fall free down your..." He stopped before he said, "your naked back," and simply said instead, "Your back."

"I'm not sixteen," she said with some asperity. "I'm thirty-one."

"So old?" He laughed. "I'm thirty-six. The age difference is good, yes?"

For what? she almost asked. But did not. Instead she said, "There's a car close behind us."

"Saoud. He doesn't trust me out alone."

"He doesn't want anything to happen to you."

"I know. He's a good man. He was with my father and now he is with me."

"Where is your father?"

"In the desert with the Bedouins. Since his semiretirement he prefers to live there." He slowed to turn into the street where she lived. "Some day I'll take you into the desert so that you can meet my father and my people."

"I doubt that I'll be here long enough for that."

"A year," he said, looking at her. "That's long enough for almost everything."

He stopped the car in her driveway and turned off the ignition. The car that had been following them slowed, then took the driveway that led to the back of the house.

"I hope you enjoyed the evening in spite of the brief disturbance." Kumar rested an arm on the back of the seat.

"Yes, I did. Thank you." Josie edged toward the door.

"We will see each other again soon." It was a statement, not a question.

She opened her door. He said, "A moment please," and hurrying around to her side he took her hand to help her out. When she stood beside him he did not release her hand but instead brought it to his lips. He kissed the back of it, then turned it and rested his lips against the inside of her wrist.

"I can smell your perfume here," he said in a voice so low she could barely hear. "I can feel the beat of your pulse against my tongue."

"Let me go."

He released her hand and stood facing her. Before she could move away he encircled the back of her neck. The skin there was smooth and cool to the touch. He curled a tendril of her hair around his fingers before his hand crept up to stroke her cheek and run the ball of his thumb across her lips.

She trembled at his touch and stepped back, dazed by a confusion of emotions.

"It has only begun between us, Josie," he said. "Never doubt that some day we shall finish what we have started. Be assured, you will not leave until it is done."

She couldn't answer, she could only stand there, frozen.

He turned away from her and clapped his hands as he called out, "Zohra! Karma!"

When they appeared in the open doorway, he said, "Miss McCall will retire now. Please see to her needs."

He took Josie's hand in his, and as he had done before, he turned it and brushed his lips across her palm. When he released her he said only "Good night," then turned and got into his car.

Chapter 7

The following morning, accompanied by her secretary, Sarida Barakat, Josie drove to the Civil Hospital. She wore a tailored dark blue dress, matching heels, and observing the custom of women who covered their hair, a small-brimmed blue hat.

As he had the night before, Saoud rode in front with the driver. Today he wore a robe of a dark saffron color. His head was covered by a clean white scarf and he wore sandals. When they pulled up in front of the three-story hospital he stepped out to open her door and said, "Prince Ben Ari has asked that I make sure every courtesy is extended to you today and that you are shown whatever it is you wish to see."

His smile, as always, was gentle. But his jaw was firm. He was going into the hospital and heaven help the man who tried to stand in her way.

The lobby was plain. And noisy. Men crowded around a reception desk, their voices raised to try to get the attention of the harried male attendant behind it. Other men, one with a bandaged head, another with his leg in a cast, sat talking on the benches that lined the wall. It was a scene of confusion, with a noise level that belonged on a football field rather than in a hospital.

Josie looked around and shook her head in disbelief, then turned to see a man in a white robe hurrying toward her.

"Missus," he called out, raising his voice so that he could be heard. "Is Missus McCall, yes?"

"Yes," Josie said. "I'm Miss McCall."

"We are at your service, most honored lady. I am Ahmed al-Shaibi, hospital administrator. Please to come to my office and we will have tea."

"Thank you, Mr. al-Shaibi, but I'd really prefer to see the hospital first."

"The women's ward. Of course, of course." He took a handkerchief out of the pocket of his robe and wiped his forehead.

"Why don't we start with the men's ward?"

"The men's ward?" He took a step backward. "Ah, but Missus, that would not be proper."

"Mr. al-Shaibi..." Josie tried for a pleasantly firm expression. "I'm here as a representative of the International Health Organization. It's the health and well-being of your patients that is important to me, not their sex."

"But Missus, you cannot..." He shook his head. "No, no, I'm sorry but I'm afraid it is not permissible for you to enter the men's wards."

Saoud stepped forward. From his height of seven feet he stared down at the smaller man. "Miss McCall is here at the request of Prince Ben Ari," he said. "She will go anywhere and see anything she chooses to see in the hospital. Do you understand?''

''But, but, but...'' Ahmed al-Shaibi cleared his throat and mopped his face. ''This is most unusual. A woman has never—''

''And she will begin in the men's wards,'' Saoud said.

Al-Shaibi took another swipe at his face with the already damp handkerchief. ''Very well,'' he said, reluctantly. ''Come along. But it is most unusual. Most unusual.''

With Sarida Barakat and Saoud by her side, Josie made her way through the hospital corridors to the private rooms and the wards on the first and second floors. Saoud kept pace a step behind Josie, and Sarida, her face averted and gazing neither right nor left, brought up the rear.

Despite the chaos below, it was quiet on this floor. Out of ten private rooms, only one was occupied. Three of the six wards were empty, but the other three looked clean and the patients seemed well cared for. Al-Shaibi introduced her to two of the doctors and several of the male nurses, all of whom seemed shocked that a woman had ventured into an all-male domain. She checked out the operating room and the X-ray equipment and all in all was impressed with what she saw.

But when she climbed the stairs to the third floor where the women patients were cared for, it was a different matter. A nurse wearing a dark gray robe greeted them. ''We were told you were coming, *madame*,'' she said by way of greeting. She looked up at Saoud and shook her head. ''It is not permissible for you to enter here,'' she added.

''I will wait at the desk,'' he said to Josie. ''If you have need of something you will call out, yes?''

"Yes," Josie said, deciding she might as well get used to the idea that as long as she was here in Abdu Resaba, Saoud would be her ever-present shadow. With a smile and a nod she turned to follow the nurse into the wards.

In her early years in nursing she had heard horror stories of the crowded county hospitals of the 1920s. That's what the wards on the third floor were like. Only worse. There were no private rooms, only three wards filled to overflowing with patients.

Mothers with newborn babies were side by side with tubercular patients. A very old woman, obviously suffering from dementia, prattled and gestured wildly, oblivious to the pain of the young girl in a body cast in the bed next to her.

Josie moved from ward to ward, sickened and made furious by what she saw. When she left the last ward she turned to the nurse who had conducted her on the tour. "This is terrible," she said, barely keeping her voice under control.

"I know that, *madame*." The woman, who looked to be in her middle fifties, wore a harried expression. Deep grooves of fatigue marred her face, and her eyes were red from lack of sleep. "We do what we can," she said with a tired lift of her shoulders. "I have only three nurses and myself."

"Three nurses for each shift."

The woman shook her head. "No, *madame*, for the entire twenty-four hours."

"There are how many patients in each ward?"

"Twenty-five, *madame*."

"All the beds are filled?"

The nurse nodded.

"So there are four of you to take care of seventy-five patients twenty-four hours a day."

"That is correct. Two on the day shift, two on the night shift. Also a cook and her helper to prepare the food."

"Your food doesn't come from the same kitchen as that of the men patients?"

The nurse shook her head. "We are cut off from the rest of the hospital in every way, *madame*. The only exception is when there is to be an operation."

"How often does a doctor see these women?"

"Dr. Nazib comes three times a week. If there is an emergency, we try our best to reach her." The nurse looked down at her scuffed shoes. "But it is not always possible."

Josie smothered an oath. She told herself that she must act like a professional. She had enough experience to know that you did not walk into a country and be the know-it-all American bent on changing the way things were done. Change took time and patience. You had to be cautious about stepping on anybody's toes. But this was outrageous!

"What is your name?" she asked the nurse who had escorted her.

"I am Jumana, *madame*."

"My name is Josephine."

Josie offered her hand and after a moment's hesitation the other woman took it. With a frightened look, she said, "You are not pleased with what you have seen. You will go to Prince Kumar and tell him how bad it is here and I will be removed from my position and punished."

"I will tell Prince Kumar what the situation is here, yes. But believe me, Jumana, you won't be dismissed, nor will you be punished for something that isn't your fault. I'll return tomorrow and with your help and the help of your nurses we'll begin making improvements. Meantime I'd like you to separate the patients with tuberculosis from the other patients. If there's not a place to isolate them, put them in the hall until tomorrow. By then I hope to have something worked out."

"I hope you can, *madame*." The nurse shook her head. But this is all the space we have. I don't see what you can do."

Josie rested a hand on the other woman's shoulder. "I'll be back tomorrow," she said. "Believe me when I tell you that things are going to improve."

She turned away and under her breath murmured, "Or I'll damn well know the reason why."

"I want to go to the palace," she said to Saoud. "Right now."

The tall man raised an eyebrow. "But you do not have an appointment, *madame*."

Josie's mouth tightened. "Now," she said.

"It is the custom for one to make an appointment if one wishes to see the prince. Perhaps tomorrow—"

Josie got into the car. Her back was straight, her chin was firm. "I must see Prince Kumar today," she said. "If I have to wait until midnight, I'll wait. But I *will* see him."

Saoud lifted his shoulders and with a nod got into the front seat. "To the palace," he told the driver. And there was in his voice just the barest hint of amusement.

But the amusement faded when they merged with the city traffic. As he had the night before, he became instantly alert, as if suspicious of each car that passed.

And again, Josie wondered why. But only for a moment. She was far too intent on what she was going to say to Kumar. Raise royal hell, that's what she was going to do. How dare he allow the women of his country to exist in the conditions prevalent in the women's wards of the hospital? Had he so little regard for the opposite sex that he would sanction such an abomination?

By the time the car pulled up to the palace entrance she was consumed with righteous indignation. To Saoud she said, "Please tell Prince Kumar that I'm here and that I want to see him."

"Yes, *madame.*" Again there was just the faintest trace of wry amusement in his voice. He led her, followed by her nervous secretary, into the entrance patio, then through a series of corridors and into a marbled reception room. "If you will wait here I will speak to the prince."

"Thank you, Saoud."

He touched his forehead, then turned and disappeared behind a velvet hanging of purple drapes.

Sarida picked at her robe. "His Highness will not be pleased," she whispered. "I am told that when he is upset he is fierce as a lion. It is not the place of women to argue with men. It is the will of Allah that we be subservient."

Josie smothered an oath and wished to God she'd never set foot in the country. But now that she had, she was going to do the job she'd been sent to do. She would clean up the women's wards at the hospital or know the reason why.

Saoud appeared through the velvet drapes. Once again he touched his fingers to his forehead, and said, "Prince Kumar will see you now, *madame.*"

When she rose, Sarida said, "Go carefully, Miss McCall. Do not anger him."

Josie only nodded. Saoud held the drape back, then led her through a tiled corridor to a gold-encrusted door.

When he opened it he grinned and said, "May Allah protect you, *madame*."

Chin up, Josie sailed into the room.

Prince Kumar, dressed in a royal blue robe, rose from behind a desk to greet her. "This is a most pleasant surprise," he said.

"A surprise perhaps, but I doubt it will be a pleasant one."

"Oh?" He motioned her to a chair. "What is it? Has something upset you?"

"Yes something has upset me. I've just come from the hospital."

Kumar waited.

"It's a disgrace," she said hotly. "An abomination!"

"Abomination? Surely you exaggerate. I myself have seen the hospital. I found the wards as well as the private rooms quite acceptable."

"The *men's* wards. Have you been upstairs to where the women patients are?"

"Of course not."

"*Of course not!*" Josie stood and leaned across the desk, so angry she wanted to throttle him. "There are four nurses to take care of seventy-five women—twenty-four hours a day. That means only two nurses to care for them on a twelve-hour shift. I saw patients with tuberculosis in beds next to newborn infants, demented patients in the same ward with terribly ill women."

"I didn't know conditions were that bad."

"Believe me, they are."

"Then we must do something."

"Damn straight!"

"I will speak to my minister of public health."

"When?"

"When?" He looked puzzled.

"When will you speak to him?"

"We have scheduled a meeting at the end of the week."

"That won't do. I want action now."

"Now?" Kumar leaned across his desk. His dark eyes were suddenly threatening. "Are you attempting to tell me how to conduct the affairs of my country?"

Josie hesitated. She knew now that she was treading dangerous water, but she had treaded dangerous waters before and they didn't scare her. On the other hand, she'd come on pretty strong. If she pursued this line of attack, she might lose everything. And she couldn't lose; the health of too many women was at stake.

"No," she said carefully. "I'm not telling you how to run your affairs of state, but I am telling you that what I have seen today in your hospital is a disgrace. I honestly can't believe that you knew such conditions existed."

Her anger forgotten with the need to explain how really bad the conditions were and how much she wanted to rectify them, she said, "I know how to help, Kumar. I know what we can do to make the women's section of the hospital function as well as the men's. If you could only see for yourself how bad things are, I know you'd want to do something about it."

He looked at her, his dark eyes intense. Then without a word he sat down and reached for the phone. "Connect me with the minister of health," he said. A moment passed. "Hamid? Is that you? I hope I'm not interrupting, but Miss McCall, whom you met last night, is in my office and she is most anxious to speak to you about our hospital. I'd like to suggest that the three of us meet at nine tomorrow morning for a tour of inspection.''

He listened for a moment, then coldly said, ''I used the word *suggest,* Hamid. Perhaps I should change that to *order.*'' He looked across the desk at Josie. ''Yes, nine. Thank you, Hamid.''

He put the phone down and to Josie he said, ''Are you satisfied?''

It was more than she had expected, so much more that she didn't know what to say. ''Yes,'' she said. ''And I...I'm sorry that I interrupted your work.'' She rose and offered her hand. ''Thank you for seeing me, Prince Kumar. And thank you for your interest.''

''I love my country,'' he said. ''Though you may find it hard to believe, I want what is best for all of our people.'' His lips quirked in a smile. ''Even for our women.''

Josie smiled back, and encouraged said, ''I think I can make a difference during the year that I'm here.''

''A year?'' He shook his head. ''That's not very long, considering all of the things I'm trying to change in my country. But we shall see, yes?'' He came around the desk. ''I'm glad you were angry enough to insist on seeing me.'' He took her hand and brought it to his lips. ''Now you will allow me to see you safely home.''

''That's not necessary.''

''And perhaps you will invite me in and offer me a cup of tea.''

''Prince Kumar—''

''Only Kumar, yes?'' Before she could object he took her arm, and when they left the office and went to where Saoud waited he said, ''I'm going to accompany Miss McCall to her home, Saoud.''

''Very well, *Sidi.*''

''Where is Miss Barakat?'' Josie asked.

"I sent her back to the consulate, *madame*. She was nervous and I thought it best. I hope you don't mind."

"No, of course not, Saoud. I'm glad you did."

"Then we are ready." Kumar, still holding Josie's arm, led her back through the corridors to the entrance where the car waited. He got into the back seat with her; Saoud sat in the front with the driver.

Josie leaned against the seat as they started off. She had been surprised by Kumar's reaction to her statement about the conditions in the women's section of the hospital. She had expected the anger which he'd shown at first, even some kind of action once he'd cooled down. But she honestly hadn't expected him to move so quickly.

"There is a problem ahead," Saoud said, breaking in on her thoughts. "It appears to be a street demonstration of some kind."

Kumar sat forward in the seat. "Can we go around it?"

"I'm afraid not, but we will try to turn." Saoud said something to the driver, who started to back up. But just as he did a crowd of people rushed forward from the side street and blocked the car from behind.

Saoud grabbed the car phone. "This is Prince Kumar's car," he said quickly. "We're blocked by a street demonstration and need help. Quickly!" He put the phone back and pulled an automatic pistol out of his robe. "The police will break this up," he said to Kumar. "It will only be a matter of a few minutes."

"What is it?" Josie sat forward in her seat. "Why are they demonstrating?"

"There's been some political unrest for the last month." Kumar's expression was grim. "Kadiri is the one who's stirring everything up. I bet anything he organized this." He, too, reached inside his robe and pulled out an automatic. "I'm sorry you had to see this, Josie," he said. "But don't worry. We're safe in the car and the police will be here momentarily."

A shout rang out and a cry went up. "It's the prince! That's his car!"

The crowd that had blocked the street ahead of them turned and rushed forward, fists raised, placards held aloft. Someone shouted, "It's Prince Ben Ari! Get him! Get him!"

"We want Kadiri!" another voice cried.

"Kadiri!" the crowd began to chant. "Kadiri."

A shot was fired. The rat-a-tat-tat of a machine gun sounded close by. Someone hurled a rock at the car. Then another and another. The window next to Josie shattered. With a cry of fear she shrank back against the seat, but before she could do little more than gasp, Kumar pulled her to the floor. Then he was on top of her, shielding her with his body.

She heard other shots from within the car and knew that Saoud and the driver were shooting. They jumped out. The doors slammed.

All around them now there were curses and shouted threats, and the terrifying screams of a mob gone mad.

The car began to rock from side to side. Over Kumar's shoulder she saw angry faces pressed against the window. A man with a baseball bat hit the window and she screamed.

"Stay down." Kumar held her, covering her body with his own as a spray of shattered glass fell upon them. The car rocked and men struck again and again at the windows.

She clung to Kumar. She remembered all the pictures and television coverage she'd seen of a mob gone wild, of men, their faces twisted with rage as they pushed forward, trampling women and even children underfoot.

Like this crowd. Frenzied, beyond control. She knew the terrible danger they were in. Knew that if help didn't come soon...

Over the scream of the mob she heard sirens. She tried to rise, but Kumar said, "No, don't move."

Guns were being fired all around the car. There were screams and cries. More sirens.

He tightened his arms around her. His face was inches from hers, his mouth was so close she felt his breath upon her cheek.

He said, "It will be over in a moment. Stay where you are." He tried to shift his weight. "Am I too heavy?" he asked. "Am I hurting you?"

Josie shook her head. She could feel the outline of his body against hers, the line of his shoulder, his hips, his legs. So close. So close...

"Josie?" The irises of his eyes went from dark brown to smoldering black, the pupils grew large and dark as a desert night.

She felt the breath clog in her throat because she knew he was going to kiss her. Because she wanted him to kiss her.

"Don't," she whispered. "Please..."

He took her words, he took her breath and the sounds of gunfire faded. There was only Kumar, the touch of his lips on hers and the feel of his body covering her, shielding her.

Her arms crept up around his neck and with trembling fingers she touched the fine curl of hair there and the smoothness of his skin. In the deep recesses of her mind she knew she should free herself, yet she did not. He shifted his weight against her and when she felt his hardness against the thin fabric of her dress she moaned a soft whisper into his mouth.

"Sho-zee," he said against her lips.

He held her close and kissed her with a passion so fierce it left her breathless. She clung to him, not even aware that she whispered his name again and again. Or that she lifted her body to his. Or that she moved against him in heated desire.

She heard the rasp of his breath. She felt the terrible tension of his body.

From outside the car came the sound of machine guns and the shouts and cries of wounded men.

It didn't matter. Nothing mattered in this moment of heated passion.

Kumar raised himself up and looked down at her, nostrils pinched, eyes narrowed with all that he was feeling.

"Some day..." He had to struggle to get the words out. "Some day we'll finish this," he whispered. He kissed her hard and fast. And let her go. "Stay where you are," he cautioned. "Don't move until I tell you it is safe."

Then he was up, and with the gun in his hand he rushed out of the car.

Josie lay where she was, breathing hard, trembling with a reaction that had nothing to do with fear. All she could think about was Kumar, and the way it had been when his body had lain over hers.

Chapter 8

Josie was in shock, too stunned by what had happened to take it all in. The car they were riding in had been riddled by bullets and the windows were smashed. The street was littered with debris, storefronts were battered, windows were broken. Men with bandaged heads stumbled past. Others more seriously wounded were taken to the waiting ambulances. Still others were dragged to the police cars.

Now that it was over, tremors of reaction started her shaking. She saw a bullet hole in the window near her head and knew that if Kumar hadn't acted as quickly as he had she might have been killed.

Kumar. She swallowed hard. It seemed almost incomprehensible that with everything going on around them, with bullets flying, rocks being thrown, a mob that at any moment might have dragged them from the car, they had come very close to making love.

My God! What was the matter with her? Had she taken leave of her senses? One touch, one kiss, and her body had caught fire. Had he been right when he'd said there was something magic between them? She'd never been like this before, had never lost control of herself the way she did with him. Even now she was far more disturbed by the closeness they had shared than she was by the terrible violence of the mob.

Kumar was everything she detested in a man. He was a macho chauvinist in a society she wanted no part of. Yet there was something about him she could not deny, an attraction she had sensed from the moment she had first seen him in the immigration line in Los Angeles. The first time he'd kissed her she had responded with a force that had shocked her. A few moments ago her reaction had been one of a primitive hunger, unlike anything she had ever known.

What in the hell was happening? Every time Kumar touched her her hormones went on a rampage. If she didn't do something about them—about *him*—she'd find herself living in a harem!

He turned and looked toward the car, and when he saw her watching him he said something to the policeman and hurried toward her.

"Are you all right?" he asked. "You're not..." He looked at her hand. "My God!" he said. "You're bleeding!"

She looked down at her hand. It was bleeding. There was blood on her arm, on her dress.

"Why didn't you tell me?" Kumar took a clean handkerchief from his robe and gently wiped away the blood so that he could see the wound. When she winced he closed his fingers over hers.

Her dress was bloodstained, one sleeve was torn. She had a scratch on her face and her hair had come loose from the chignon. Filled with a tenderness he had not even known he was capable of feeling, he said, "I'm so sorry you had to witness such a demonstration, Josie. Sorrier still that you were hurt."

"It's only a scratch." She withdrew her hand from his. "I'm all right, really."

"We'd better have a doctor check it."

"I'm a nurse," she said, managing a smile. "Believe me, Kumar, it isn't serious. I'll take care of it as soon as we're back at my house."

The injured driver was being taken to the hospital in an ambulance, so Saoud drove. Kumar sat in the back beside Josie. A police car was positioned in front of them; another followed behind. When they reached Josie's Kumar helped her out of the car and into the house.

He took her into one of the downstairs bathrooms and bathed her hand. The inch-long cut between her thumb and first finger had stopped bleeding. Although Josie protested that she could take care of it, he wouldn't let her. He washed her hand with soap and water and applied an antiseptic. When she winced, he felt a stab of pain and sucked his breath in.

What's happening to me? he asked himself as he bandaged her hand. Why does she affect me this way? What is there about this one woman that causes me to feel as I do?

The thought crossed his mind that perhaps he should send her back to her own country where she would be safe. But almost as soon as the idea formed he rejected it. He couldn't let her go. Not yet.

He took the hand he had bandaged and gently kissed it. "I'm so sorry you were hurt," he said.

"It's nothing. There's no need to make a fuss."

"We were in a dangerous situation," he said. "If anything had happened to you I would never have forgiven myself."

He called for her servants, and when Karma came he said, "Your mistress has been hurt. Help her to bathe and to change."

And to Josie he said, "Perhaps you'd feel better if you rested for a little while."

"I feel fine, Kumar. I don't need to rest. I'm perfectly all right."

He wanted to touch her again but knew that he should not, certainly not in front of the servant girl. So he said only, "Very well. I'll wait here until you return."

When he was alone he went to the phone. He ordered that three of his personal bodyguards be assigned to watch Josie's home night and day. And when he had summoned Saoud, he said, "You'll sleep here in the house from now on. When she goes out you'll go with her. Don't leave her side."

The tall man nodded. "Have no fear. I will protect the woman with my life."

"I know, my friend. I trust no other man as I trust you."

Kumar's next call was to Aubrey Bonner. When he had been assured that there had been no disturbance at the consulate and that all was secure, he said, "I am going to have extra guards posted immediately. If there's trouble of any kind notify me at once."

"Now," he said to Saoud when he put the phone down, "we must see to Kadiri."

"If it was he who instigated the riots, then I pray Allah will see that he suffers a long and lingering death staked out over a sand dune in the noonday sun with fire ants crawling over him.''

"It's a pleasant thought, Saoud, and we'll do our best to see that it comes to pass. But first we have to prove that he was behind what happened today."

"Give me one afternoon alone with him and you will have your proof."

Kumar smiled grimly. "Much as I would like to, I cannot accede to that. But I will investigate, and if he is—as I suspect—behind these demonstrations, I'll take the proper measures. He won't get away with what he's done, Saoud. Of that I will assure you."

Josie came into the room. Instead of the tailored clothes she usually wore, she was dressed in one of the robes Kumar had purchased for her. It was of green silk, and as Kumar had hoped, it matched the color of her eyes. Her skin was rosy from her bath. She wore no makeup and her hair hung in soft waves over her shoulders.

Unable to take his gaze from hers, he said to Saoud, "I've asked for extra guards to be sent to the consulate. Will you see that my order is being carried out?"

When the other man left the room, he said to Josie, "Come, let us have a brandy," and indicated the alcove off the living room.

It was dimly lighted by the lantern that hung from the filigree ceiling. It looked cool and dim and strangely seductive. She hesitated, but Kumar took her hand and led her to the blue velvet sofa.

When she had first seen the alcove, she had wondered if lovers had ever made love here. Now the thought brought a feeling of unease.

Kumar opened a chest, took out a bottle and two crystal glasses, and when he had poured a bit of brandy into each of them he came to the blue sofa and handed one to her.

"This will help," he said, and touched his glass to hers. When he drank he said again, "I can't tell you how sorry I am about what happened today. I'll understand if you want to return to your own country, but I hope you won't."

He held his breath. If she said she wanted to leave, he wasn't sure what he would do. He had to gamble that she wouldn't walk away until she had done the job she had been sent to do. Nevertheless, it was a risk.

Josie took a tentative sip of her drink. "I admit that I was spooked by what happened today, but no, Kumar, I don't want to leave—at least not until I've straightened things out at the hospital." She put her glass down on the table. "I haven't thanked you for protecting me today. I do—thank you, I mean. You very likely saved my life."

"If I have, then I must be—according to our tradition—henceforth responsible for your well-being." He reached for her hands. "It will be a task I won't take lightly, Josie."

The small alcove with the shaded lantern light and the lingering smell of incense seemed to be closing in on her. Kumar's eyes held hers. She cleared her throat, and striving for a lighthearted answer, said, "That's okay. I hereby release you from all obligations."

"What if I don't want to be released?" He moved closer, and taking her injured hand in his, said, "It's time for both of us to stop denying that there is something between us, Josie."

"What...what happened before, in the car I mean, was because of..." She shook her head as though trying to clear it. "It was because of the danger, Kumar. It heightened our…our feelings. Our emotions. But that's all it was.''

"I don't think so." He moved closer, so close that he could smell the clean, fresh scent of her skin and the fragrance of her hair. "And in California?" he asked. "Was there danger there when we kissed?" He shook his head. "No, Josie. The only danger then was the danger of your lips."

Before she could move away, he cupped her chin and kissed her. He felt the intake of her breath, the softening of her mouth, and though she did not answer his kiss, she did not try to move away from him.

He took her hands in his and drew her up beside him. "Do not doubt that some day what we feel will be consummated, Josie. It's our destiny." He kissed her again, and against her lips he said, "When it happens, I will make love to you as no one ever has before."

"Don't…" She swayed against him. "Please… Let me go."

He stepped away from her. "For now." He rested his hand on the top of her head and curled the soft tendrils of her hair around his fingers. "I'll call for you tomorrow morning and we will go to the hospital. If there's anything you need in the meantime, you need only ask. I'll speak to the cook and ask her to prepare a light meal for your dinner tonight. When you have finished, you will rest, yes?"

He kissed her again and his mouth was warm on hers. Then he let her go and hurried out of the room.

When he left Josie sank down to the blue sofa and closed her eyes. "Kumar," she whispered, and trembled because she did not know what tomorrow would bring.

*   *   *

Hamid Mizra was as broad as he was tall. His gray-streaked hair looked as if it had been blown dry by a wind machine. His mustache was shaggy and he had a nose that made every other feature shrink in comparison. His teeth were large, his smile obsequious.

He and Ahmed al-Shaibi were waiting for them when Kumar and Josie arrived at the hospital.

"Prince Kumar," Mizra said with great enthusiasm, "how good it is to see you. And you Miss McCall. A pleasure, indeed a great pleasure."

Josie acknowledged the greeting. "Shall we proceed?" she asked. "I'd like to start with the men's section."

Mizra raised his eyebrows. "You mean that *we*—" he indicated Kumar and al-Shaibi "—we *men* will proceed to the men's section of the hospital."

"No, Mr. Mizra, that isn't what I mean." She started toward the stairs.

Mizra didn't move. "Surely, Prince Kumar," he said, "the American lady does not intend to go into the men's section of the hospital."

"I'm afraid she does," Kumar said.

And though there was a part of him that did not approve of her take-charge attitude, he could not help but admire Josie's spirit. She was here to do a job, and by Allah, she was going to do it, in spite of him, Mizra and the devil himself, if she had to.

He had never been to the hospital before, but had relied instead on Hamid Mizra. The minister of health had assured him that the institution was as up-to-date as any hospital in the civilized world. And indeed, when Kumar, following behind Josie, inspected the men's wards and private rooms, as well as the operating room, it seemed to be.

"Now," Josie said, when they had completed that part of the tour, "we'll inspect the women's section."

"Ah, *madame,* I'm afraid we cannot do that," Mizra said. "It would not be proper to enter the domain of women."

"You've never been up to the third floor?" Kumar asked.

"Of course not, Prince Kumar. But I have been assured—"

"By whom?" Kumar asked.

"Well, by...by Ahmed al-Shaibi, of course. Yes, yes, I have been assured by him that the women patients are just as well cared for as the men."

"No, they're not!" Two bright spots of color appeared in Josie's cheeks and without another word she started up the stairs.

Kumar motioned to Mizra and al-Shaibi. "After you, gentlemen," he said.

The nurse that Josie had seen yesterday met them when they came in. When she saw Kumar, she touched her fingers to her forehead and bowed. "Prince...Prince Kumar Ben Ari. I did not expect ... I did not think that you yourself would do us the honor..." She looked at Josie as though for assistance.

And Josie said, in her careful Arabic, "Prince Kumar and Minister Mizra would like you to show them the wards, Jumana."

"But they are men," the nurse whispered.

"If you would, please," Kumar said. "We want to see everything."

The nurse, with a nervous twitch of her mouth, motioned the two men ahead of her. Josie followed behind. She didn't speak or offer a comment. Kumar stopped at many of the beds and spoke to the patients. Mizra said nothing. His face had reddened, his mouth was tight. He looked neither right nor left.

When the tour ended Kumar thanked Jumana and the other nurse in attendance, and the three of them, along with a silent and obviously nervous Ahmed al-Shaibi, made their way down the stairs and into al-Shaibi's office.

When they were seated and hot mint tea had been served, Kumar turned to Josie and said, "I'd like to hear your suggestions."

She opened her purse and took out the notes she had made the night before. "Three of the wards on the men's floors are empty. Only one room of the ten private rooms on those floors is occupied. I'd like to take over one section of the second floor, two of the wards there and five of the private rooms and have them converted for women patients."

"But that cannot be done!" The hospital administrator jumped up out of his chair. "Impossible," he declared. "Quite impossible."

"Sit down, al-Shaibi." Kumar turned to Josie. "Go on," he said.

"At least six other nurses have to be hired and there must be a doctor in attendance or on call twenty-four hours a day. Another thing—the women are served their meals from a different kitchen. I haven't inspected it or the other kitchen that prepares food for the men's wards, but I have a feeling that the women's kitchen is as inadequate as everything else on the third floor. That has to be rectified as soon as possible."

"Very well," Kumar said without hesitation. "You'll be in charge. I'll see to it that you have whatever help you need."

Mizra cleared his throat. "If you will forgive me, Prince Kumar, I believe that I should be the one in charge."

"It should have been your job all along, Hamid. But since you have not done anything to improve the conditions of the hospital, I'm leaving all of this up to Miss McCall. I will, of course, expect you to assist her."

"Me? Assist *her?* But she is a woman. What you ask is quite impossible."

"Then I'm afraid I must ask for your resignation."

Mizra half rose out of his chair. "Excellency, I—"

"Effective immediately," Kumar said. And dismissing his minister of health he turned back to Josie. "I'm sure Mr. al-Shaibi will let you and Miss Barakat share his office and that he and his staff with assist you in every possible way."

"Of course." Al-Shaibi took a handkerchief from his robe and wiped his brow. "Anything you say, Prince Kumar. Anything Missus McCall wants. Of course. Of course."

Kumar smiled. "Then it is arranged. She and Miss Barakat will be here tomorrow and you will offer them every help and every courtesy."

And al-Shaibi, obviously terrified by what had happened to Hamid Mizra, said again, "Of course. Of course."

When they were in the car, Josie said, "Thank you, Kumar. I guess there's something to this prince-of-the-royal-family business, after all."

"Damn straight," he said, with a grin, using one of her expressions. "But don't think that what you have undertaken will be easy. I've given the order that the hospital staff is to assist you, but that doesn't mean you won't meet with opposition. You're a foreigner and a woman. The next few weeks will be difficult.''

"I've handled difficult situations before." She settled back against the black leather seat. "I can handle this one."

"Yes, I believe you can," he said with a smile.

The next four weeks were the most difficult of Josie's professional career. Though she received lip service from al-Shaibi, in reality he did little to help her. The most help she received came from one of the two male doctors on the staff. He had done residency work at the Henry Ford Hospital in Detroit and at Johns Hopkins, and though he still held to many of his country's traditions, he agreed with Josie that the situation in the women's section of the hospital was truly abominable.

With his help and the help of his male nurses, Josie was able to move the three tubercular patients into one of the private rooms on the second floor. After that was done she began converting three of the empty men's wards into a women's section. In order to do that a wooden partition had to be built dividing the floor so that the men and women would never see or be in contact with each other.

Sarida Barakat helped her find five nurses, and Josie hired, in addition to Dr. Zahira Nazib, a young woman doctor from Morocco.

She did not see Kumar during this time, but she knew from rumbles among the hospital staff that there was growing unrest in the country. She had seen the anti-American scrawlings on the walls and fences: "Down with the United States." "Kill the infidels!"

Several times she found it necessary to speak to Kumar on the phone, and when she did he was always available. When once she asked about the problems of political unrest, he brushed them off, saying, "The situation is not as serious as it seems. Kadiri has gone into hiding, so at least he is no longer working from within the cabinet."

"I've seen the signs," she said. "About the United States."

"Pay no attention to them. There are a few rabble-rousers, but we are rousting them out. Soon we'll have Kadiri, and when we do this will stop."

Several times he asked her to have dinner with him. Each time he did, Josie refused.

"I spend most of my mornings at my office in the consulate," she said. "By noon I'm at the hospital, and I'm usually there until very late. When I finally get back to my residence I'm too tired to do anything."

That was all true, of course, but it was not the real reason she didn't want to see Kumar. The truth was that she needed time to sort out how she felt about him.

She had come to respect him as the provisional leader of his country during his father's absence. And certainly she was grateful for his having backed her up on the hospital issue and giving her a free hand there.

But on a personal level she held back. When her work here was finished she would return to her own country. Any thought of a relationship with Kumar was unthinkable.

That's what Josie told herself.

But sometimes at night when she lay alone in her bed she thought of him. And of how it had been for that brief span of time when, in the heat of battle, he had covered her body with his.

* * *

She got along well with Aubrey Bonner. He was a career state-department man, and although he took his job seriously, neither he nor Ed Petersen had bothered to learn the language of the country, as she had. For one hour every day Sarida Barakat gave her lessons in Arabic, and every night before she went to sleep Josie studied the next day's lesson. She still had a long way to go, of course, but she was learning.

During her second week in Abdu Resaba, Edith Petersen called to invite her to lunch. In spite of Josie's busy schedule she knew, according to protocol, that she had to accept. She did, but as far as she was concerned, the luncheon was a disaster.

When one of the servants, a girl who could have been no more than twelve or thirteen, dropped a plate while clearing the table, Mrs. Petersen jumped from her chair and shouted, "You stupid cow! Pick that up at once and get out of my sight."

She'd gone on and on, then, about the ignorance of the people. "The country is run by men," she said. "Macho chauvinists who believe the only function of a woman is to serve and service them. They keep them robed and veiled, barefoot and pregnant."

With plump beringed fingers she drummed the pristine white cloth. "My God," she'd said. "These damned Arabs. I can't wait to get out of here."

Josie had been appalled. But later, when she returned to her own residence, she realized that she herself had voiced the same words—macho and chauvinist.

That gave her pause. Was she, in her own way, as

prejudiced as Edith Petersen? Had she, even before she had come to Abdu Resaba, formed an opinion of its people? Of Kumar Ben Ari?

So it was that the next time he called to invite her to have dinner with him she accepted.

Chapter 9

Because he thought Josie might be more comfortable in a restaurant than in one of the private dining rooms of the palace, Kumar had his secretary make reservations at the Royale Jamai. There was a show there he had seen when he'd entertained some Texas oilmen. They had enjoyed it, and he thought Josie might find it entertaining.

Instead of the limo he drove one of the convertibles, and when he arrived to pick Josie up, Saoud frowned and said, "It would have been better to have used the limousine, *Sidi.*"

"With the royal crest on the side?" Kumar shook his head. "No, Saoud, the convertible will draw less attention. After all, my friend, this is supposed to be a date, not a state occasion."

"I will, of course, accompany you."

"You will, of course, *not.*"

"But, *Sidi*—"

"No buts, Saoud. I wouldn't take Miss McCall out at night if I didn't think it was safe."

"I will follow behind."

"I'd prefer you didn't."

"I'd prefer I did."

"*Zfft!*" Kumar exploded, and with hands on his hips, glared at the tall man. It would do no good to argue. For years Saoud had been his father's right-hand man, and when his only son had been born he'd turned much of the raising of Kumar over to Saoud.

Saoud had wiped his nose when he was a child, accompanied him to Paris when he'd attended the Sorbonne and to Beirut when he went to the university there. He had counseled him through numerous love affairs and been by his side in battle. Saoud was a second father, the best friend a man could have, and Kumar had learned a long time ago that it did no good to argue with him once he made up his mind.

"Very well," Kumar said. "Follow us, if it will make you feel better."

With the slightest of smiles, Saoud touched his fingertips to his forehead and bowed. "As you wish, *Sidi*. I will tell Miss McCall that you are here."

She came into the room, and as it happened every time he saw her, Kumar felt a catch of breath in his throat. Tonight she was wearing a blue sequined jacket and a long blue skirt with a slit that came to just above her knee. Her hair was back in a chignon. She wore pearl earrings and a single strand of pearls.

And though the pearls were all right, he found himself thinking, star sapphires. That's what she should be wearing.

The night was warm, the sky studded with stars. "You
don't mind having the top down?" he asked when he
held the door for her.

"No, it's a beautiful night."

"I hope you're hungry." He pulled out of her driveway onto the road. "I haven't asked you if you like our
food."

"I like what I've had so far."

"Tonight you must sample everything." He turned to
smile at her. "You're a bit thin, you know. We must try
to fatten you up."

"For what?" she asked with a lift of her eyebrow.

Kumar smiled. "Who knows?"

The Royale Jamai was set half a mile back from the
road amid a stand of palm trees. It was a magnificent
white-and-gold building, glittering with lights. Tall black
men wearing bright red robes and tasseled fezes took
care of the arriving cars.

Once inside the gold-and-white building, Kumar and
Josie entered into what looked like the lobby of an opera
house. The robed man who met them there said, "Good
evening, Prince Kumar. How delighted we are to see you
again." He led them across the lobby to a large brass-
encrusted door and motioned for Josie to enter what
looked like a very large Bedouin tent.

The lights were low and through the dimness she saw
that instead of regular tables and chairs there were sofas big enough for two, with a table in front of each sofa.
The setting was beautiful, intimate and quietly seductive.

"Come." With a hand on Josie's elbow, Kumar followed the other man to one of the candlelit tables and
seated her into a soft, deep sofa.

"We will have champagne," he said, when he settled himself beside her.

"This is . . ." Josie looked around her in wonder and shook her head. "A little overwhelming."

"I thought you might like it."

"I do. It's like something out of the *Arabian Nights* or a 1940s movie. I half expect Humphrey Bogart or Peter Lorre to be lurking in the shadows." She beamed a smile. "It's beautiful, Kumar. Thank you for bringing me here."

He smiled back, pleased that she was pleased, and knew he had been right to bring her here rather than to the palace.

The champagne was served. He touched his glass to hers, and when the orchestra began to play he rose from the sofa and held his hand out to her.

"Come and dance with me," he said.

For a moment Josie hesitated, remembering how it had been the night they had danced at the rehearsal dinner at the Hotel Del Coronado in San Diego. But because he had not released her hand, she let him lead her to the dance floor.

At first she held herself stiffly, but his arms were warm and strong, and little by little she began to relax. Tonight he had worn a robe in a light tan color, of a material that was as smooth as cashmere. With his dark-as-the-night black hair, deep brown eyes and skin the color of golden sand, he reminded her of Omar Sharif in *Lawrence of Arabia,* in that breathtaking moment when Sharif had ridden into view out of a haze of misty sand.

He moved with the sensuous grace of a jungle cat. In the dimly seductive light of the dance floor, it seemed as if the other couples faded away and they were alone. The muscles of his shoulder rippled beneath her fingertips.

She felt the pressure of his thigh against hers, the press of his body.

He brushed a kiss on her temple and she caught the scent of musk on his skin. The hand against the small of her back began to move in slow concentric circles, warming her as he urged her closer. And though she told herself she should move away, she did not. Instead her fingers crept up to the back of his neck, to feel the soft curl of hair there, to caress his heated skin.

When the music stopped they were in the shadows, away from the hanging brass lamps that offered what little light there was. Still holding her, he whispered her name, "Josie . . . Sho-zee," and gently kissed her.

"The music has stopped," she whispered.

"I know." His face was close to hers. "But I don't want to let you go." He kissed her again and this time his gaze lingered on the décolletage at the opening of the blue jacket. "You're so lovely," he whispered. And brushed the tips of his fingers across the rise of her breasts.

Her eyes drifted closed and a sigh shivered through her.

And through him before he let her go.

When the waiter came, Kumar ordered ripe canta-loupe served with salty slices of feta cheese, a salad of greens mixed with tomatoes, black olives and fresh mint, and artichokes cooked with lemon and saffron. That was followed by pigeon wrapped in thin, layered pastry, roast lamb cooked with dates, and rice and steaming chicken couscous.

They sipped champagne while they waited for the food to be served, and though Kumar asked her to dance again, she refused. It was too dangerous. Being close like that unsettled her.

She had told herself after the day of the riots, the day when he had covered her body with his and she had wanted him with a desire that made her ache every time she thought about it, that she would never let anything like that happen again. She had to remember that she had come to Abdu Resaba against her will, that Kumar had paid three million dollars to bring her here. It was a lot of money, but she wouldn't be bought.

He was handsome, sexy, and he could be incredibly kind. But the fact remained that he had forced her to come to his country. They were two entirely different people; she musn't allow herself to succumb to him or to the emotions raging inside her.

When they finished dinner, though Josie protested she couldn't eat another bite, he ordered baklava for dessert.

When it was served, he took a small piece and held it to her lips. "Taste," he said. "You will like."

The pastry, layered with nuts and coated with honey syrup, was deliciously sweet.

"Another bite," he coaxed, and when she had taken it he brushed his thumb across her lips and whispered, "Taste."

Held by his gaze, unable to look away, she slowly licked the taste of honey from his thumb. A spark of flame quivered through her.

"Kumar," she said, and he kissed her.

His mouth was warm and as sweet as the pastry had been.

"The baklava is good?" he said against her lips.

"Oh, yes," she said. "Oh, yes."

He held another piece to her lips and when she had taken it he kissed her again, and this time she tasted the sweetness on his lips and on his tongue.

The spark of flame became a fire. "Don't do this," she whispered.

He let her go. "I'm sorry," he said in a voice so low she could barely hear. "I know this is neither the time nor the place, but something happens to me when I am with you. I want to kiss you in ways I have kissed no other woman, touch you in ways I have not touched them. I want to do things with you I have only dreamed of doing." He took a steadying breath. "Forgive me," he said. "I should not say these things."

They moved a little apart, but he kept his arm around her shoulders and took her hand in his.

A small band made up of zithers, a piping horn and a thin-skinned drum began to play a kind of music she had never heard before. It was different, strangely exotic.

A snake charmer appeared with a round wicker basket. He sat cross-legged on the floor, and after he had removed the top of the basket, he began to play a flute. A cobra rose from the basket and started to sway to the thin, high music.

When another snake appeared, uncoiling as it came, flat head darting right and left, tongue flicking in and out, Josie moved closer to Kumar.

"Do not worry," he whispered, and tightened his arm around her.

The cobras faced each other, heads darting, tongues flicking as they swayed to the music in a strangely hypnotizing *danse macabre*.

Half afraid, half fascinated, Josie watched the writhing serpents. This was unlike anything she had ever seen, and like so many things in this country it was so foreign, exotic. And yes, erotic.

When at last the snake charmer left, the music changed and a belly dancer appeared. She was veiled.

Her sheer costume was covered with golden coins, sequins and bangles that glittered in the spotlight.

She began slowly, moving with sensuous grace, swaying her body as the serpents had done, moving to a rhythm so obviously sensuous that Josie felt hot color flood her cheeks. The beat quickened. The dancer's hips rolled and the muscles of her stomach moved round and round.

The men sitting close to the stage leaned forward, eyes intent, hands beating to the rhythm of the dancer. Faster, yet faster she moved to the beat of the drum and the piping of horn.

She fell to her knees, body arched back, waist-length hair flowing behind her, arms raised, sweat-slick body undulating to the beat until in a wildly frantic burst of music it was over. She lay still for a moment, supine, full breasts heaving with effort, then rose and with a bow to the crowd, fled from the stage.

"Well," Kumar said. "How did you like the dance?"

"I'm not sure. I think she was very good."

"Yes, she was." His fingers tightened around her shoulders. "What else? What of the dance itself?"

"It's very…" She hesitated. "Provocative," she said. "I can see why men like it."

"Yes, we do." He laughed, and then his face sobered. "Sometime, Josie, when it is the right time, I would like you to dance for me." He touched her hair. "When you do, your glorious hair must be free. You will wear a veil that is sheer enough for me to see the beauty of your face. And a gossamer gown so that every inch of your body will be revealed."

For a moment she was too shocked by his words to speak. When she could she said, "You…you musn't say things like that to me, Kumar."

"You're wrong, Josie. I can say them *only* to you. But if you are offended, then I apologize and ask your forgiveness." He signaled to a waiter and asked for the check. When it came and he had put some bills on the table, he rose, and taking Josie's hand he led her out of the restaurant.

His car came, and behind it a darker car with Saoud at the wheel. Kumar helped Josie in, and with a nod toward Saoud, went to his side of the car.

They spoke little on the way to her residence. Once there he escorted her to the door and into the inside patio. The air was filled with the scent of lemon blossoms and the moon cast silver shadows on the water bubbling from the white marble fountain.

"I hope you've had a pleasant evening," Kumar said. "I hope, too, that I didn't ruin it by being too forward."

"No," Josie said. "But we can't..." She shook her head. "You mustn't say such things to me, Kumar. You shouldn't kiss me."

He put a finger against her lips. "If there is one thing I *should* do, it is to kiss you." He cupped one hand around the back of her neck to bring her closer. "There is something between us, Josie, something neither of us can deny. I don't know what it is, and perhaps like you I am trying to pretend that it doesn't exist. But I know that it does, just as I know that some day we will be together, for however long or brief a time."

He kissed her and his lips were cool on hers. He took her lower lip between his teeth and ran his tongue back and forth across it before he eased his tongue into her mouth.

His mouth was warm. So warm. He pressed her closer and with a smothered gasp she began to answer his kiss, touching her tongue to his, holding him as he held her.

When he let her go, he cupped her face between his hands. Looking deep into her eyes, he kissed her again and said, "Think about this tonight when you are alone in your bed. Think of how it will be when finally our bodies join as one."

He let her go and stepped away. "Good night," he said. "Sleep well."

When he had gone Josie stood alone in the patio, breathing in the scent of the lemon trees, watching the moon dapple the silvered water of the fountain.

And knew that he was right. For though she would try not to, tonight she would think about him and of how it would be if they ever made love.

The next day he sent her a star-sapphire necklace with matching earrings.

There was growing unrest in the city. A riot broke out in front of the palace. It was quickly brought under control, but on the following day there was an even bigger riot right at the entrance of the American consulate.

More demonstrations followed. Placards called for the downfall of Sheikh Rashid Ben Ari and of his son, the prince. Rabble-rousers from a faction led by Sharif Kadiri incited thieves and malcontents. Spies infiltrated from the country of Azrou Jadida. Under cover of night, arms were smuggled across the border.

It was a time of unrest and of danger. When Josie called Kumar to say that she could not accept the star sapphires, he said, "We'll talk about it later. I've called an emergency meeting of my ministers and I'm late. I've only a moment, Josie, but I want to urge you not to leave your residence for the next few days."

"But I have so many things to do," she protested. "Both at the consulate and at the hospital."

"Delay them. I have a feeling things in Abdu Resaba are going to get worse before they get better."

She heard another voice, and Kumar said, "I really can't talk any more. I'll call you when I can."

She put the phone down. Kumar had asked her not to leave her residence, but he was being overly cautious. Saoud accompanied her wherever she went and usually another car followed behind. Yesterday, when she'd left the hospital, an angry street gang had surrounded their car. But the gang had backed off as soon as Saoud and the men in the other car pulled their weapons.

The work she was doing at the hospital was important. She couldn't back off, not now.

She was pleased with the way things were shaping up. Perhaps by the end of the week she'd be able to spend less time there and more at the consulate. But right now she had to be at the hospital.

Dr. Nazib, now that she had finally been given the authority that was due her, was an enormous help. As was the head nurse, Jumana. Together the three of them, with the assistance of the other nurses, were turning the women's section of the Abdu Resaba Hospital into an institution the country could be proud of.

In a week or two Josie would visit outlying clinics, but preparations had to be made before she did. Meantime, she struggled to get the hospital running the way she wanted it to.

By the end of the second week she was able to begin spending her mornings at the consulate catching up with the needed paperwork, and her afternoons and evenings at the hospital.

She was at the consulate the morning it was attacked.

She had been in Aubrey Bonner's office and was just starting out the door with a sheaf of papers in her hand when the first explosion hit.

The force of the blast knocked her to the floor. She lay there, badly shaken, too stunned for a moment to move.

Behind his desk, Bonner, his face ashen, his black suit white with plaster dust, cried, "Are you all right?"

"I ... I think so. What happened? What ... ?"

Another explosion ripped through the building. Windows shattered and blew. One section of the wall split and crumbled and fell into the room.

"My God!" Bonner stared at her, unbelieving. "We're under attack!" He grabbed the phone. "Get me the palace!" he shouted. "Hello? Hello? Can you hear me? This is Bonner at the consulate. We're being attacked. I must talk to Prince Kumar."

Gunfire cracked. Josie dropped to the floor just as a spray of bullets ripped through the broken windows and into the room.

"Stay where you are!" Bonner ordered.

She waited a moment, then started to her feet just as another explosion hit. It knocked her down, choked her in the dust of crumbled plaster.

My God! she thought. They're bombing the building.

Bonner screamed into the phone, banged it, jiggled the receiver. "Damn!" he cried. "Damn it to hell, we've been cut off!"

There was a terrible pounding on the consulate door, frenzied cries of, "Get them! Burn them out. Death to the foreign infidels!"

Josie and Bonner stared at each other. "I've got to see if any of the others are hurt," Josie said, scrambling to her feet.

"No, no, you musn't." He half rose out of his chair, but before he could stop her, she ran out of the room.

The hallway was littered with debris, the door to her office was ajar. She ran in. The office was a shambles. One wall had caved in. Her desk chair had smashed halfway through a window. Part of the ceiling lay atop her desk. Her secretary's desk slanted at a crazy angle. "Miss Barakat!" Josie cried. "Are you in here?"

When there was no answer, she ran around the broken desk, and saw Sarida Barakat on the floor, unconscious, a fallen beam across her legs.

"Sarida!" She knelt beside the other woman and felt for her pulse. It was thready, irregular. The woman's face was gray and cold to the touch.

She had to get the beam off her legs. She tried to lift it, heaved and tugged and knew she couldn't do it alone.

She ran into the corridor, crying, "Help! I need help! Somebody..."

An explosion hit. It flung her against the wall amid flying glass, and like a broken doll she slid slowly down and slumped to the floor.

Kumar was at his desk when his phone rang. He picked it up and his secretary said, "Prince Kumar! The consulate is under attack!"

"What? What? Is Bonner on the phone?"

"We were speaking when there was an explosion and we were cut off. Shall I call out the army?"

"Immediately. And a helicopter. We may need it to get those people out of the consulate." He hung up and dialed the hospital. "Miss McCall," he snapped. "Is she there?"

"No, sir," one of the nurses answered. "She phoned to say she would be at the consulate this morning. Is there anything I can . . . ?"

He dropped the phone. "Josie!" his mind screamed. "Josie!"

Flanked by police in riot gear and two open trucks filled with soldiers, Kumar sped through the streets toward the consulate. An armed mob tried to block the car he was in. His soldiers began firing. The rioters fired back. Men screamed and fell wounded as the army trucks and police cars advanced.

Kumar, armed with an Uzi, leaned out the window of his car, and though one of his men said, "Get down, Prince Kumar," he did not take cover.

He heard the terrible roar of explosions and knew the rebels were using incendiary rounds, maybe even rocket launchers. His mouth went dry with fear.

Amid gunfire his car pushed through the street. When it turned a corner he saw the consulate. Part of the roof had been blown off. Flames shot up. Walls were down.

As he watched, horrified, a man in the crowd fired a 40-mm grenade launcher. Before he could fire another, Kumar jumped from the car and fired his Uzi. The man screamed, but it was too late. The first grenade launcher had found its mark.

"Hurry!" Kumar shouted as he jumped back into the car. "Hurry!"

"The helicopter," the soldier next to him said. "It's trying to land on what's left of the roof."

Kumar looked up. The helicopter hovered for a moment, then cautiously settled on the section of the roof that hadn't been destroyed.

As men spilled from the army trucks, his car sped toward the consulate door. Before it stopped, Kumar was out and running up the steps. His guards came behind him, shouting, "Wait, Prince Kumar. Wait!"

But he paid them no heed as he found the stairs leading to the second floor. He raced up them two at a time and when he reached the top he saw that the destruction was even worse on this floor. He ran past fallen beams until he reached the stairs leading to the roof, and burst through the door.

They were getting into the helicopter; Bonner, Petersen and his wife, two of the secretaries.

"Miss McCall?" he cried. "Josie? Where is she?"

"I don't know." Bonner ducked low and hurried toward him. "She was in my office when it started, but she left. Wanted to see if anybody was hurt."

"Damn it, man!" Kumar clenched his fists. "Didn't you try to find her?"

"I had to get my files," Bonner said. "Confidential papers. I couldn't leave them behind."

He staggered and Kumar realized he'd had a blow on the head and that he was bleeding. "All right," he said gruffly, and taking Bonner's arm hurried him to the helicopter.

Petersen and his wife were already aboard.

"I've got to take off," the pilot called out.

"Not yet," Kumar said. "Not until I find Josie McCall."

"No!" Edith Petersen screamed. "I want to go now. I'm a citizen of the United States. I demand—"

"Please, Edith," her husband tried to say. "We can't leave without Miss McCall."

"Shut *up!*" She struck at her husband's chest. "Get us out of here! Get us out of here!"

Kumar stared at her. He turned and looked toward the stairs. Where was Josie? In the name of Allah, where was she?

"I've got to take off," the pilot yelled. "If I don't do it now I won't be able to make it."

Kumar felt the heat of the flames and knew the pilot was right.

He looked back at the door, hoping...hoping against hope he would see her. But there was no one. He turned to the pilot. "Go!" he shouted, and sprinted for the stairs.

She tried with all her strength to get the board off Sarida Barakat's legs. She tugged and lifted until she saw black spots in front of her eyes. She cursed and pushed and cried. She screamed for Saoud, for Bonner, for Petersen. Nobody heard her, nobody came.

She knelt beside Sarida. She felt her pulse and knew it was weaker. "God," she said under her breath. "Somebody. Help me. Help me."

The terrible shooting went on, but the explosions had stopped and so had the battering at the door. She smelled smoke and knew she had to get out before the walls caved in and the roof fell.

But she couldn't leave Sarida, she had to do something. Had to. Had to.

She got to her feet again and tried to lift the beam. "Move, damn you," she said under her breath. "Move."

* * *

Kumar climbed over fallen beams and piles of debris. Half blinded by smoke, he ran into an office, saw the tilted crest of the United States and knew it was Bonner's. He ran out and down the hall. Saw an open door and started in.

Josie! Her dress was torn, her face was dirty. She had a bump on her forehead and cuts on her arms. She was struggling with a beam, trying to lift it, muttering words he hadn't known American women used.

"Josie!" he cried.

She turned. Her eyes went wide with shock. "Sarida," she said. "She's hurt. Help me..." And with a strangled cry she slumped to the floor.

Chapter 10

It seemed as if she had been sleeping for a week. Now and again she was roused by a woman robed in white, who spooned hot tea or soup into her mouth. And once she opened her eyes and saw Kumar beside her bed.

"Sarida," she managed to say. "Miss Barakat?"

"Her legs are broken, but she's going to be all right." He closed his hand over hers. "So are you, Josie. You've had a concussion and some cuts, but the worst is over. All you need to do now is rest." He stroked her forehead. "Sleep now, my *laeela*," he said. "Sleep now."

When she awoke the next time her head, though it ached, felt clearer. There were scratches on her left arm and a small bandage on her right wrist. Other than that she seemed to be all right. But she didn't know where she was. This certainly wasn't like any hospital room she had ever seen.

Pale apricot curtains moved in the breeze that came in from the open French doors. There were satin sheets on her bed, a bowl of gardenias on one of the bedside tables and a bouquet of pink roses on the dresser. A velvet chaise had been placed in front of the French doors near a table and two chairs.

She raised herself up on the white satin pillows and saw that she was wearing a pink lace nightgown. What in the world...?

She threw back the satin coverlet and swung her legs off the bed, but before she could rise the door opened and the robed woman she had seen before entered.

"No, no." The woman hurried into the room. "You are too weak. You must not get up alone." She helped Josie back into bed. "I am Fatima. When you want me, you have only to ring this." She indicated a silver bell on the nightstand.

"Where am I?"

"In the palace, *madame.* When you were hurt, Prince Kumar brought you here."

"The palace? And Miss Barakat? Is she here, too?"

"No, *madame,* she is in the hospital."

"How long have I been here?"

"It is four days now."

Four days? Josie put a hand to her head as though trying to clear it. The last thing she remembered was trying to lift the beam off Sarida's legs. There had been noise and smoke, and she'd been terribly afraid that she couldn't save Sarida. Then, like a dream, she had seen Kumar. That was the last she remembered.

"I'll tell Prince Kumar you are better," Fatima said. "When you have bathed, I will bring your breakfast."

"I can manage alone."

"No, *madame,* you cannot. If you were to fall and hurt yourself again the prince would..." The woman stopped and with a chuckle said, "At the very least he would have me boiled in oil. Therefore, because I know you would not want that to happen, you will allow me to be of assistance, yes?''

And so it was that when Fatima had run a bath she helped Josie up and into a room that looked more like a tropical garden than a bathroom. Recessed behind the pink marble tub was a forest of plants and flowers; baby orchids of every hue, Madagascar jasmine, frangipani blossoms, ferns. On the ledge of the tub she saw the scent she used alongside a display of French bath oil and soap, soft pink washcloths and towels. A dressing table stood at one side of the room. The ceiling was mirrored.

She let Fatima help her down the marble steps into the tub, but when the woman picked up a washcloth and a bar of soap, Josie said, ''No. I can bathe myself.''

''You are sure, *madame?*''

''Quite sure.'' With a wave of her fingers, Josie motioned the other woman away. When she was alone she lay back in the warm water and looked up at the mirrored ceiling. This was a long, long way from Bakersfield, the California town where she'd grown up.

The scented water rose around her. She closed her eyes, remembering.

Her father had owned a gas station in Bakersfield, her mother had been a nurse. When Josie entered Santa Cruz on a partial scholarship, her parents helped as much as they could. And she'd helped herself with part-time jobs at the campus bookstore and a pancake house. The bookstore had given her a ten-percent discount on her books; the pancake house had kept her in pancakes and waffles.

Her grades were good and in her senior year she had applied to and been accepted at Stanford Medical; her lifelong dream was coming true, she was going to be a doctor.

But her dream had been smashed by a drunken driver on the curving mountain road above Big Sur. Her father had been killed in the accident, her mother so badly injured they hadn't expected her to live.

But Ellen McCall had lived, for a year, and by that time there'd been nothing left of the Stanford fund both she and her parents had saved for.

With her dreams of medical school behind her, Josie had entered nurse's training. If she'd had moments of regret, she never spoke of them. She loved nursing and with International Health she'd traveled to places she had never expected to see. Hopefully she had left each medical facility a little better than it had been before she'd come.

But of all the countries she had seen, of all the places she had lived, none had been as exotic as Abdu Resaba. And though she still resented the way Kumar had forced her to come, she was glad now that he had. The hospital was shaping up. As soon as she was able she would visit the outlying clinics. If, and it was a big if, after what had happened at the American consulate, she was allowed to stay on.

It all came back to her then, the attack, the bombing, the fire, her own desperate efforts to free Sarida. And the certain frightening knowledge that she would not have left the other woman to perish in the fire. If Kumar hadn't found her... But Kumar had found her. She was in the palace of a prince, which at the moment seemed a pretty good place to be.

When Josie finished bathing she washed and dried her hair and slipped into the thick terry-cloth robe that had been placed on a chair next to the tub. There were toiletries on the dressing table; lotions and creams, combs and hairbrushes, bath powder and scented lotions, all obviously new.

She had finished arranging her hair and was perfuming her skin when Fatima came in with a green silk caftan over her arm, a pair of silk bikini panties and a thin wisp of a bra.

"There are other clothes in the closet," the woman said when Josie had dressed. "Come, let me show you."

She led Josie back into the bedroom and opened the mirrored doors at the opposite end of the room.

There were robes and caftans of every fabric and color; pale greens, delicate pinks, lavender, burnt orange, ivory, light blue, dark blue. And neatly arranged on racks on the floor dozens of pairs of satin slippers in matching hues.

"And here," Fatima said before Josie could recover, "are your underthings."

She went to the dresser and began to open drawers that displayed all manner of swim wear and underwear; satin panties, lacy bras, provocative teddies and nightgowns.

Josie looked at the frivolously expensive display, not quite sure whether to be angry or amused. "These aren't mine," she said at last. "My clothes are at my residence."

"But these are also yours, *madame*. Prince Kumar had them flown in from Paris."

Flown in from Paris? What was going on here? She couldn't accept such gifts. Besides, she had her own things back at the house he had provided for her.

Josie looked at Fatima and shook her head, but before she could say anything, Fatima said, "Prince Kumar has asked me to serve dinner in your room this evening. He also asked if he could join you."

"Tell him that, yes, he may join me," Josie said with a frown, determined to tell him the minute she saw him that she couldn't possibly accept the clothes. And that tomorrow she would move back to her own place.

When Kumar came at sunset, he found her sitting in one of the lounge chairs beside the pool. "I knocked," he said. "But you didn't hear."

"It's beautiful out here in the garden."

"Yes, it is." But Kumar wasn't looking at the garden, he was looking at her. Indicating a chair, he asked, "May I?"

"Of course." Josie hesitated, for though he had overstepped in bringing her here and in buying clothes that she could not accept, he had saved both her life and Sarida's. He had been kind and concerned and she was grateful for all that he had done for her. Nevertheless...

"It was kind of you to bring me here," she said. "But I'm all right now. I'll leave tomorrow and go back to my place."

His eyebrows drew together in a frown. "That's out of the question. You need at least another week of recuperation."

"Kumar..." Frustrated, Josie shook her head. "Look," she said, "I know you're trying to help, but you shouldn't have brought me here. You shouldn't have bought me all those clothes, if they really are for me."

He smiled. "Of course, they're for you."

"I can't accept them, Kumar."

"Nonsense. You have to wear something."

"I have my own clothes back at the residence you provided."

"But you're not there," he said reasonably. "You're here. While you are, you'll wear the clothes I have provided." He paused. "They're not to your liking?"

"Of course, they are. They're beautiful, but—"

"Then, they are yours. As for your returning to the other house, I'm afraid that's impossible—at least for a while. Dr. Nazib has said that while your wounds are not serious, you need time to recuperate."

"I could go to the consulate." She hesitated. "Surely it's being repaired and there is still a part of it that's livable."

"The consulate has been destroyed," Kumar said. "Mr. Bonner and Mr. Petersen, along with Mrs. Petersen, have left Abdu Resaba."

"They've left?" Josie stared at him. Her eyes went wide with shock. "Where... where are they?"

"They returned to the States the day after the consulate was attacked. I'm sorry, Josie, but at the moment there is no United States consulate in Abdu Resaba."

No consulate? But if there was no consulate then she was in Abdu Resaba without the protection of her country. "You..." She wet her lips. "You arranged for them to leave?"

"They were airlifted by helicopter directly to the airport. Mr. Bonner suffered a minor wound and was treated there."

"Ed Petersen was all right?"

Kumar nodded. "Neither he nor his wife were injured."

"And they left right away, directly from the airport?"

"With Mrs. Petersen loudly voicing her disapproval of my country." His voice grew mock serious. "I debated about whether or not to let her leave, for though she wouldn't have brought much of a price on the slave market, six months in a harem under the supervision of a stern taskmaster would have done much to improve her disposition."

In spite of her growing concern over her own fate, Josie grinned. She had a sudden vision of Edith Petersen, dressed in flowing veils, surely flowered, being turned this way and that as an auctioneer rattled off her dubious charms. When the vision faded, so did the grin. If the others had gone, then she would soon be leaving too. In a strange way, she wasn't sure how she felt about that.

"When am I to leave?" she said.

"You're not."

"I . . . I beg your pardon."

Kumar leaned forward. "The airport has been closed. I could have you flown out in my private plane, but it would be risky because you'd be flying over enemy territory."

He hesitated then, wondering how much he should tell her. "We're almost in a state of war, Josie. The riots have stopped, but there is the smell of danger in the air. The army is on alert and the air force is on standby. We know that Sharif Kadiri is behind all of this, and we believe he's gone to Azrou Jadida to gather forces for an attack."

"An attack?" Hand to her throat, Josie stared at him.

"Yesterday, I received word from my father. He is rallying the Bedouins to fight with us. If we have them, we will win. Meantime, believe me when I say that you are safer here than you would be if you tried to leave the country.''

''There isn't any other way I can leave?'' she asked. ''I mean other than by air?''

Not quite meeting her gaze, Kumar said, ''No, I'm sorry. It's impossible.'' And he did not tell her that there was a way across the desert to Saudi Arabia.

The day she had walked away from him in California and told him how she felt about Middle Eastern men he had decided that one day he would have her exactly where he wanted her, in his country, on his turf. ''You're like Aiden,'' she'd said. Aiden, the man who had beaten and abused her friend. Without knowing him, she had grouped him with such a man. She had insulted him and all the decent men of his race and blood. And because she had, he had made up his mind that some day he would have her exactly where he wanted her.

''You'll be quite comfortable here in the palace,'' he said. ''Fatima will be at your beck and call.'' He smiled and took her hand in his. ''And so will I.''

''No,'' Josie said with a shake of her head. ''If I must stay in Abdu Resaba, then I will live in the house you have provided for me.''

''I'm afraid that won't be possible.''

She stood and looked down at him. ''Why not?''

''You wouldn't be safe there.'' He, too, rose, and facing her said, ''You're an American citizen, Josie. And because you are, Sharif Kadiri would love to get his hands on you. It's up to me to make sure he doesn't.''

''Kadiri? But why?''

''To hold you for ransom or...'' He hesitated. ''To auction you off to the highest bidder.''

''You're...you're joking,'' she said.

''Am I?''

She stared at him. His face was impassive, serious, strangely cold.

It hadn't occurred to her that she might be in danger, or that if civil war broke out she would be trapped here in Abdu Resaba.

"Please don't look so worried," he said. "I won't let anything happen to you."

He brought her hand to his lips and kissed it. She felt the warmth of his breath against her skin. And knew somehow that the thought of a civil war was far less dangerous than being here in the palace with Prince Kumar Ben Ari.

They had dinner on the patio overlooking the pool. Fatima served champagne with the hearts-of-palm salad, white wine with the fish, red with the couscous, and dark Arabian coffee with the baklava.

When the other woman put the plate of baklava between them, Josie looked at it suspiciously. The last time she'd had the sweet dessert Kumar had fed it to her, bit by luscious bit. She didn't want that to happen again and so she said, "I've had enough. I really couldn't eat another bite."

"Then we will wait a while, yes?" He got up, and crossing to Josie's chair, took her hand and led her to one of the chaises. "You'll be more comfortable here," he said. "We will have our coffee and dessert, and you will relax."

Relax? Not likely. Not with a full moon rising over the royal palms and the scent of jasmine and orange blossom drifting on the evening air.

He motioned to Fatima, who had been waiting at one side, and said, "When you have cleared the dishes you may go. I will serve the coffee and dessert."

He took the chaise next to Josie's. In a little while Fatima left, and they were alone in the moonlight.

"Have you ever been in the desert?" he said into the silence.

Josie shook her head. "I don't like hot weather."

"You get used to it." He handed her a cup of strong Arabian coffee. "There's a magic about the desert," he said. "Once you have been there it becomes a part of you, bone and blood of you, and when you are away there is place in your soul that longs to return."

He took his coffee, and after he had added a teaspoon of sugar, leaned back in the chaise and looked up at the sky. "The temperature cools at night and there are so many stars it seems that the heavens are filled with celestial light. On a night like this, with a moon like this, the sand turns the color of gold. A breeze comes in off the desert and it smells..." He shook his head, searching for the words to describe the place he loved most in the world. "It smells of desert heat, of sun and sand, of meat roasting over hot coals, camel dung and leather. On such a night you forget the heat of the day."

He put his cup down and turned to her. "I'll take you to the desert and you will see for yourself why I love it."

Josie shook her head. "I'd hate the heat. I'd hate the loneliness."

Kumar swung his legs off the side of the chaise. "But you wouldn't be lonely, because I would be with you," he said softly.

"Kumar—"

"No, do not tell me you will not go, because you will. Some day we will be together in the desert, and I will teach you to love it as I do."

He picked a piece of the baklava off the table. "You have not eaten your dessert," he said. "One small bite, yes?"

"No, I . . ." She shook her head. "No, thank you. I don't want any."

"I wonder why it is you always say no to me?" He moved to sit beside her on the chaise, and when he leaned close he brushed the small piece of the sweet pastry against her lips.

His face was close. His dark eyes were lighted by moonlight. She wanted to tell him not to do this, because she did not want to feel what she had felt that night in the restaurant. But he held the baklava to her lips and looked at her with his dark desert eyes. Her pulse raced, her body softened and she ate the baklava from his fingers.

Fingers that lingered and touched her lips with a gentle stroking motion.

"It is good, yes?"

"Yes." Barely a whisper. "Yes."

He gave her another small piece and brushed his fingers against her lips again, and when he did she took the tip of his finger between her teeth. She gently bit and held him there as she ran her tongue back and forth across it.

He closed his eyes and a shudder ran through him. When he opened them he took the cup of coffee out of her hand and drew her into his arms.

"I have wanted to kiss you from the moment I walked out here tonight," he said.

His mouth was tender. He licked her lips, tasting the baklava and her. He touched his tongue to hers, searching, sampling, and when she moaned into his mouth he tightened his arms around her.

She told herself she must not let him do this, but made no move to escape.

The kiss grew, deepened and became a silken duel of tongue twined against tongue. He held her so close she could feel the frantic beat of his heart against her breast.

Draw away, a voice inside her head warned. In a moment, she told the voice. Only a moment.

He eased her back against the chaise, and still kissing her, kicked off his sandals and lay down beside her. The length of their bodies touched, mouth against mouth, breast against breast, hips, legs. Warmth coursed through her. Heat. Desire.

He cupped the back of her head. He whispered her name against her lips. "Josie, my Josie."

No, she wanted to say. Not yours. Never yours. But she could not move away because she was a prisoner of his arms, held by him, kissed by him, returning his kisses with her hungry mouth, holding him with her needy arms.

When he cupped her breast she put her hand on his wrist to draw him away. But he said, "Let me touch you like this. I need to touch you like this."

His fingers were like fire against the thin fabric of the caftan, moving in a circular motion while his thumb rubbed the already hardened nub.

"Oh, please," she whispered. "Please."

"Please what?" With his hand still on her breast he raised himself on one elbow.

"Don't," she said.

"Don't touch you like this?" He gently squeezed the rigid peak between his fingers, then bent and through the fabric of her gown he kissed the place his fingers caressed.

She felt the heat of his breath, and when he took the tip of her breast between his teeth she cried out and her body yearned and twisted against his.

He drew her closer. He put one hand against the small of her back and pressed her to him so that she could know and feel his desire.

She began to tremble, and with both hands against his shoulders, tried to free herself. He wouldn't let her go. He held her there, so close that it was as if their bodies had already joined. He kissed her and took her breath.

She tried once more to push him away. Tried and failed. And moved her body against his in slow, heated motions.

When he raised his mouth from hers he cupped her face between his hands. "If we don't stop now, I will not be able to stop. Do you understand?"

She could barely breathe, but she managed to say, "I...I know."

"Is this what you want?"

Tears like drops of morning dew rose in her eyes. She leaned her head against his chest. "No," she whispered. "No."

"Do not weep." Still holding her face, he kissed the tears that rose and fell. Then he let her go, and rolling away from her, lay on his back and looked up at the stars.

Josie had responded to him in a way that set his blood on fire. For now he knew, no matter what she did or said, that she felt as he did. He knew, too, that one day she would come to him willingly. The day she did, he would have won. Then and only then would he be able to let her go.

Let that day come soon, he thought in a silent prayer to Allah. Let it come soon.

* * *

She stood at the French doors after he left, looking out at the pool and the chaise where they had lain. Her breasts were swollen, and though she was naked her skin burned as with a fever.

A sigh quivered through her and with a strangled cry she raced to the dresser and pulled out one of the bathing suits. When she had put it on she stepped onto the patio and ran to the pool. She sat on the edge for a moment, then took a deep breath and lowered herself into the water.

She swam until she was gasping for breath. Only then did she lean her arms over the edge of the pool, panting, exhausted.

When at last she pulled herself up and out of the pool she stood looking out toward the lights of the city and the desert that lay beyond.

Kumar's desert.

She sighed and a shiver of fear ran through her, fear of the unknown, of him, and of the emotions she felt whenever she was with him.

There beside the pool, with water running down her body, her hair streaming down her back, she cupped the breasts that ached for his touch. And ran her fingers over lips that he had kissed. Kumar, her heart cried. Kumar.

From the balcony of his room he watched her turn and go toward her room. "Josie," he said. And knew that soon she would be his.

Chapter 11

Rashid Ben Ari was an impressive figure of a man. As tall as his son, but of a broader build, his hair was thick and black and only the temples were touched with silver. He was a powerfully virile man who, before and after his only marriage—to Kumar's mother—had enjoyed more than his share of women. Even now, two years away from his sixtieth birthday, there were few women who could resist him.

Certainly Jasmine, daughter of the head of the tribe of Abedi, could not. Three years ago when Rashid had turned the running of Abdu Resaba over to Kumar and had gone into the desert to live with the Bedouins, he had met Jasmine. They had been together ever since.

Rashid had been content with Jasmine and with his life in the desert. But when word had come of the troubles in the capital, he knew he must return to be of whatever help he could to his son.

Saoud brought Kumar the news that his father had returned. "My father?" Kumar rose from behind his desk. "Show him in at once."

But before he could get to the door it opened and his father strode in.

Father and son embraced. Rashid held Kumar away from him and kissed both his cheeks. "By Allah, it's good to see you," he exclaimed.

"And you, Father."

Rashid motioned Jasmine forward. "You remember Jasmine?"

"Of course." With a smile, Kumar took the lady's hand and kissed it.

An attractive woman in her mid-forties, Jasmine Abedi seemed very small beside his father. She wore a robe, but now that she was here in the privacy of the palace, she had removed her veil. While not a classically beautiful woman, her olive skin was flawless and her dark eyes sparkled with life and intelligence.

"It's a pleasure to see you again, *madame*," Kumar said. "I trust your journey here was enjoyable."

"Three days riding a camel through incredible heat is not a pleasant way to travel, Prince Kumar. Though I am a daughter of the desert, I much prefer the city." She turned to Rashid. "If you will excuse me, my lord, I would like to take a decent shower and rest in a decent bed."

"Of course, my dear." He turned to Saoud, who had posted himself at the door. "Will you call someone to have the lady Jasmine shown to my rooms?"

"Yes, my lord." Saoud motioned to Jasmine, and when the two of them had left the room Rashid said, "I hope my coming will not inconvenience you."

"This is your home, Father. I'm overjoyed that you're here." Kumar took Rashid's arm and led him to a chair. "How are things in the desert?" he asked.

"The tribes quarrel, as always. They need a leader, someone who is more diplomatic than I am." Rashid sighed. "I know my failings, Kumar. The Bedouins need a strong hand, but a diplomatic one. I'm afraid my brand of diplomacy has me brandishing a pistol in one hand and a bullwhip in the other. It worked in the old days, but no longer. That's why I've come."

"I don't understand."

"The pistol and a bullwhip are needed here in Bir Chagga. Your kind of diplomacy is needed in the desert."

Kumar's eyebrows rose. "You want me to go into the desert?"

Rashid nodded. "I'm convinced you can do a far better job than I can in bringing the tribes together." He reached into his robe for a cigarette, lighted it and said, "You are of the desert, just as your mother was. She was Bedouin, Bedouin blood runs in your veins. They're your people, Kumar. Your heritage. You understand them far better than I ever will."

Kumar studied his father's face, then he, too, reached inside his robe for a cigarette. Five years had passed since his last long visit to the desert. He had stayed for six months, made friends and earned the respect of many of the desert chieftains. He'd ridden with them and fought beside them, and for a while at least he had felt that he was a part of them.

But that had been five years ago. How would they feel about him now? How would he feel about returning to the desert? And what of Josie? The thought of leaving her hit him like a physical pain, yet how could he deny his father?

"I haven't been there for a long time," he said.

"But you're a desert man, my son." Rashid clapped a hand on Kumar's shoulder. "Why do you hesitate, Kumar? War is coming to Abdu Resaba and we need the Bedouins. If you can bring the tribes together as one great fighting unit, we stand a good chance of winning. Without them..." Rashid shook his head. "Without them I'm not sure how much of a chance we have."

He drew in on his cigarette and through the waft of smoke asked, "What of Sharif Kadiri? Have you been able to find that bastard son of a she-camel?"

"No, father. I've had some of our best secret-service men looking for him. They're pretty sure he's in Azrou Jadida."

"Gathering an army," Rashid said with a frown.

"I'm afraid so."

"We have to be ready when he strikes. By then, with the help of Allah, we'll have the Bedouins with us. While you're in the desert, I'll be here in Bir Chagga. Between the two of us we'll wipe out Kadiri and his followers." Then, as if it were a fait accompli, he said, "When can you leave? My caravan waits at the city gates."

"There are things I must take care of first. Will the day after tomorrow be satisfactory?"

"Yes, of course." Rashid rose. "I shall see you at dinner, then?"

Kumar nodded. "I have a guest," he said. "If you don't mind, I'll ask her to join us."

"Her?" Rashid raised one eyebrow. "A woman?"

Kumar nodded. "She's an American with International Health."

"I thought all American personnel had left the country."

"She was injured when the American consulate was attacked and I had her brought here."

"I see." Rashid stroked his chin. "Yes, by all means ask her to join us. I'll leave you now. Dinner at eight-thirty?"

"Yes, Father."

"It's good to be back, my boy. And damn good to see you."

"And you," Kumar said with a smile.

He lighted another cigarette when he was alone. As the smoke wafted up to partly cover his face, his smile faded. He would do as his father asked. He had no choice. Even though it meant leaving Josie.

Fatima brought Josie the news that Sheikh Rashid Ben Ari, the father of Kumar, had arrived, and that she was to join the two men for dinner that evening.

At eight she bathed and dressed in a blue satin caftan. With it she wore the star-sapphire necklace and earrings Kumar had given her.

She had returned his gift the day after she received it, but when he had brought her here after her injury she had found the necklace and the earrings, still in the velvet box, among her underthings.

When she began to apply her eye makeup, Fatima said, "Why don't you use a bit of kohl, *madame?* Your eyes are beautiful, but with the kohl they will be even more beautiful."

Josie had never worn it before, but now with the tips of her fingers, she applied the smoky cream to her eyelids, and admitted to herself that, yes, it did make her eyes more exotic.

For Kumar? A shiver quivered down her back with the thought of him and of how close they had come to making love.

I have to leave, she told herself. And soon. For if I stay... She looked into the mirror, looked into her eyes made smoky green by the kohl, and knew that if she did not, sooner or later she would succumb to him and to the fires that burned whenever he touched her.

When she left her rooms she found Saoud waiting to escort her to one of the dining rooms. He wore a scarlet robe tonight. His head was covered by a clean white cloth and he had leather sandals on his feet.

He touched his fingers to his forehead when he saw her, and motioning her to precede him said, "Tonight you are as beautiful as the flowers of the desert, *madame.*"

"*Shukran*, Saoud," she said. And with a smile added, "And you are as handsome and as colorfully brilliant as the birds that fly in the summer sky."

His lips twitched. "I see you are learning our ways. Perhaps we will make of you an Arabian woman, after all."

"I very much doubt it," she answered with some asperity, but she was smiling when she entered the dining room and her smoky green eyes were alive with laughter.

For a moment Kumar didn't move, he only stared at her, struck by the thought that she was different each time he saw her. Tonight she was a temptress, an exotic flower in her soft blue caftan, with the jewels he had given her sparkling at her throat and in her ears. She was so beautiful she took his breath.

"You are the American." Rashid Ben Ari hurried forward, his hand extended. "My son has told me that you were injured when the consulate was attacked. But you are better now, yes?''

Josie took his hand. ''Yes, thank you.''

He led her toward the other woman in the room ''This is my friend, Jasmine Abedi.''

''Madame,'' Josie said. ''My name is Josephine McCall. My friends call me Josie.''

''Then so will I. And please call me Jasmine.''

Kumar came to join them. ''You look lovely tonight, Josie.'' He took her hand in his and kissed it, and when he lifted his gaze his eyes rested on hers, but only for a moment.

Aha, Rashid thought, so that's the way the magic carpet flies. That's why Kumar hesitated when I asked him to go into the desert. He doesn't want to leave the American woman.

He wondered if they were sleeping together. If they weren't, they soon would be. The sexual tension between them was like crackling static in the air, so alive you could almost touch it.

That's the way it had been between him and his lovely Zenobia. She had been so beautiful, so untouched, and yet so ready to come into his arms on their wedding night. They had loved each other for ten years. He had been faithful to her and when she had died a part of him had died with her.

Thinking of her brought a sadness to his dark eyes. He watched the American woman and his son trying not to look at each other, and he felt an unfamiliar longing for days that had been and were no more.

''My lord?'' Jasmine offered him a dish of dates and there was a look of empathy and understanding in her dark eyes he had not thought her capable of. For the last three years she had warmed his bed and seen to his every comfort. In his own way he loved her. Perhaps one of these days... But, no, he did not need to think about that now.

The breast of chicken cooked in water buffalo milk was delicious, and the *kuftah,* lean lamb ground with onion and parsley and spices, the best he had ever eaten.

"I have missed such food," he said, wiping his mouth. "And you, my boy, had better enjoy this while you can, for I assure you, you will not have a feast such as this when you're in the desert."

"The desert?" Josie looked across the low table at Kumar. "You're going into the desert?"

"My father has asked me to unite the Bedouin tribes, to bring them together into one strong fighting group."

"I see." She looked down at her plate, and not meeting his eyes asked, "When will you leave?"

"The day after tomorrow."

"Before you go I must know everything you can tell me about the situation here," Rashid said. "Which of the ministers you trust, the general mood of the people and whether the majority of them are for or against us. I, in turn, will tell you about the men you must deal with in the desert."

"Tomorrow," Kumar said. "We will discuss all of this tomorrow."

He looked from his father to Josie. He saw the questioning look in her eyes and knew that if he went into the desert without her she would be gone when he returned. How could he let that happen? How could he leave her?

Dinner was over. The two men lingered at the table over coffee and cigarettes. Jasmine and Josie stood at one end of the room beneath a colorful tapestry.

"It's beautiful, isn't it?" Jasmine indicated the men on horseback, white robes billowing out behind them, rifles raised, their mouths open in a shouted war cry.

"Beautiful and different." Josie brushed a loose strand of hair back over her ear. "What is it like in the desert?" she asked.

"It's unlike anything you've ever known, a kind of life that is hard too explain. My lord Rashid lives in a primitive kind of luxury. There are velvet hangings in his tent, but the floor is of sand. The days are hot and dry and you hate them, but the nights..." She sighed. "The desert nights are made for love. When the moon is full and a breeze drifts over the dunes and the air is sweet with the smell of the desert, you forget the heat of the day. And you think there is no place on earth as beautiful as this place."

"If you're with the right man?"

Jasmine laughed. "Of course," she said. "And Rashid is the right man for me." Her laughter faded and she looked over to where the two men were deep in discussion. "But I wonder sometimes if I am the right woman for him. I'm so afraid that one day he'll leave me. When he does there will be nothing left for me. It will be finished."

"You love him so much?"

"So much and more. I have lived with him in a palace and in a tent. I would go anywhere with him. I would do anything to be with him." Her gaze met Josie's. "That is the way it is when you love a man, my dear. He becomes your life, he is all that matters."

When you love a man. Had she ever felt for a man what Jasmine felt for Kumar's father? What would it be like to love with that kind of intensity? That kind of passion?

She wasn't sure she wanted to love like that. She didn't know if she was capable of giving all that she was, her heart and all of her passion to a man.

She looked at Kumar, standing beside his father. He was so tall, so handsome in his white robe. And yes, so foreign compared to anyone else she had ever known. Drawn by an invisible bond, he turned and looked at her. For a moment it seemed there was no one else in the room. His eyes met hers as though he knew what she had been thinking, as though he could look into her very soul.

I love him. The thought, like a current of electricity, emptied her of all other emotion. I love him.

But how could she? Could love exist when people were so different? It hadn't worked for Jenny and Aiden; it wouldn't work for her and Kumar. And yet... And yet...

Jasmine touched her arm. "You've suddenly gone pale," she said. "What is it? Are you ill?"

"No, I... I'm a little tired, that's all. Will you excuse me? Please tell Kumar's father and...and Kumar that I'm going to rest now."

"I will tell them." Cool fingers encircled Josie's wrist. "I do not know what has passed between you and Kumar," she said softly. "But I will tell you that love is not something to be fearful of. It is to be embraced. To give yourself to the man you love is not to lose yourself, rather it is to find the very core of your being." She smiled gently. "To love, Josie, is to know the reason why you exist, for love is everything."

Josie looked into the wide, dark eyes. "Is that the way you love Rashid?"

"Yes, that is the way I love him."

"I don't think I can love that way."

"I think you already do." Jasmine released her. "Go now and rest," she said. "I will tell the men you were tired. We will speak again tomorrow, if you like."

Josie stared at her a moment longer before she turned and left the room.

Fatima waited for her outside her door. "I won't need you tonight," Josie said. "I'm tired. I want to be alone."

She went in and closed her door before the other woman could protest. Inside she slipped the blue caftan over her head and threw it on a chair.

Once in the shower she closed her eyes and let the water wash over her. Kumar was leaving. He was going into the desert. All right. All right. It was time for her to go home, back to the States and after that to the promised job in Paris. Away from here, away from him.

Jasmine was a hopeless romantic, a woman of a different culture who was content to follow a man wherever he led, even if that man was not her husband.

But Josie wasn't an Arabian woman, she was an American. Independent. Able to take care of herself. She didn't need a man, and she was, by God, going to Paris. And damn it to hell, the tears were only because she'd gotten soap in her eyes.

When at last she came out of the shower she took a jar of scented lotion from one of the bathroom shelves. She creamed her legs and her arms and put on one of the satin nightgowns Kumar had bought for her.

Standing in front of the mirror she unpinned her hair and brushed it. Pretend time is almost over, she thought. Kumar was going away and she was going home.

When she came out of the bathroom she went to stand before the French doors. Out there beyond the mountains lay the desert, dark, mysterious and frightening. Would Kumar be in danger there? Were the tribes he was supposed to unite dangerous? So dangerous his father hadn't been able to control them. Was that why he was sending Kumar in his place?

Someone knocked at the door and she turned back from the French doors, a little annoyed because she'd told Fatima that she was tired and wanted to be alone.

When she opened the door it wasn't Fatima who stood there, but Kumar.

"You left without saying good-night," he said.

"I told Jasmine to tell you and your father that I was tired."

"Are you all right? You're not ill?"

"No, I..." Suddenly aware that she was wearing only the nightgown with nothing over it, Josie took a step back into the room. "You'll have to excuse me," she said. "I'm about to go to bed."

"I'll only keep you a moment. May I come in?" Before she could object, Kumar came into the room and closed the door behind him. "Why did you leave so suddenly?" he asked. "Did Jasmine say something to upset you?"

"No, of course not. I like her."

Kumar smiled. "Yes, so do I. She has brought much happiness to my father, and for that I'm grateful." He took a step closer. "You're very beautiful tonight, Josie."

"You shouldn't be here, Kumar," she said. "I'm not dressed."

The satin gown clung to her slender form. It cupped the rise of her breasts and outlined the curve of her hips and her legs. She was a goddess, so deliciously feminine he couldn't take his eyes off her.

She took a step backward. "You're going into the desert," she said.

"Yes."

"I'll go back to America."

"No."

"No?"

"Come with me to the desert, Josie."

"Come with you?" She stared at him. "That...that's impossible."

"Nothing is impossible." He smiled, then his face sobered. "I need you, Josie. I want you."

She held her hands up in front of her, her palms toward him as if to keep him away. But he took her hands and drew her toward him.

He put his arms around her. Her skin was smooth and scented. With a strangled cry he splayed his hands through her hair and kissed her with hunger and with need.

Slowly, slowly, her lips parted under his. Her mouth was cool and fresh and sweet. Oh, so sweet. He couldn't get enough of her. He tasted her lips, suckled and licked them. He bit the corners of her mouth and took her lower lip between his teeth. Like a man dying of thirst he ran his tongue over it, suckling, sipping of her sweetness.

He kissed her closed eyes. He breathed in the scent of her hair. His body hardened with passion and with need.

"Please," she whispered. But he didn't listen.

Her skin was silky soft, softer than the satin gown. He cupped her breasts and felt her warmth beneath his fingertips. He rubbed his thumbs across the turgid peaks and when she moaned he took the moan into his mouth. And thought he would go mad if he could not have her.

She was helpless in his arms, overcome by his kisses, lost in the feel of the hands that caressed her through her satin gown. Her skin heated, she trembled and when she swayed toward him he brought her closer, so close that through his robe she could feel his tumescence pressing hard against her.

"Make love with me," he whispered against her lips. "I need you, Josie. I need you so."

"I . . . I can't."

"Yes, you can."

"No." She could scarcely breath. "I don't know . . . I can't think. When you touch me like this . . . when you kiss me like this, I can't think."

"Then, don't." He cupped her face between his hands. "Only feel, Josie. Only feel." He drank from her lips. "You want this as much as I do, my sweet *laeela*, my sweet girl. Let me make love to you. Let me carry you to bed and show you how much I hunger for you. How much I care."

He swept her up in his arms, and with his mouth against hers to smother her protests, he carried her to the bed.

"No," she said, and struggled to free herself. "Please, don't."

He laid her down. He lay beside her. He took her mouth and kissed her with all of his pent-up longing, with all of his desire.

He urged her closer, so that the whole delectable length of her was against him. The satin was smooth beneath his hands. Her breasts were soft. The tender peaks strained against her gown, waiting for his touch.

With a cry he slipped the gown over her shoulders. Her body was even more beautiful than he had imagined. Her skin was like creamy ivory touched with the delicate shade of a rose. The tips of her breasts were small, poised, waiting.

He flicked his tongue over one and she cried out. He took it between his teeth to taste and to tease and she writhed against him. And though she tried to get away, he held her there while he kissed her breast and pressed her close, closer.

Aroused as she never had been before, her heart beat so hard she thought for a moment she was going to faint. This was heaven; this was hell. She never wanted it to stop; she knew she had to stop.

With the last of her waning strength, Josie wrenched free.

"No," she whispered. "I'm sorry. I don't want..." She couldn't go on, couldn't find the words to tell him that she couldn't do this.

He rolled away from her, onto his back, hands clenched to his sides, aching with the need to have her, tempted as he had never been tempted before to take her by force. He could. Could take her, make her. No. Damn it, no. He couldn't do that. Not to her. Never to her, unless she wanted him the way he wanted her.

They didn't speak or touch. At last he turned toward her again, and raising himself on one elbow, looked down at her. Her hair was disheveled, her face was flushed. She was trembling, vulnerable.

"I'm so sorry," she said. "I know this is terrible. I know it's unfair. But—"

"But you don't want me." He rolled away from her and got up. "I'm sorry I forced myself on you. It won't happen again. The day after tomorrow I'll be gone and you'll be rid of me."

He went to the door, but there he turned. "My father will make your travel arrangements as soon as things cool down here. Until then, of course, my home is yours."

He opened the door. "It could have been good between us," he said.

Then he was gone and Josie was alone.

With a cry she buried her face in the pillow and cried as if her heart had been broken.

As indeed it had.

Chapter 12

Josie slept very little that night. When she did, it was to dream of Kumar. He rode with the men in the tapestry... in a dream so real she could smell the sweat of the horses, hear the pounding of their hooves, and the terrible cry of the warriors as they rode headlong into battle, rifles raised above their heads, robes billowing out behind them. Kumar in front, leading them on into danger they could not see but that she knew was there.

She tried to cry out to warn him, but her voice was like the mewling of a kitten, and she awoke sitting straight up in bed, her heart beating as hard as the horses' hooves that had pounded over the desert sand.

She slept again, to dream again... She was in a tent, lying on soft deep-piled pillows. Her body felt light, yielding, yearning...

He stroked her with gentle hands and raised his body over hers. Moonlight turned his skin to gold. She stroked his naked shoulders... And awoke trembling, heated.

With a moan she pressed her fingers to lips she had only imagined he had kissed, to breasts that tingled from his imagined touch. And wept because it had only been a dream.

"When you love a man, he is a part of you," Jasmine had said. "He is your life, your love."

With her face turned into the pillow, Josie tried to blot out of her mind the way Kumar had looked when he'd said, "You don't want me."

Not want him? Dear God, her body cried out for him. Even as that sensible part of her brain whispered, "He's too different. You musn't love him. In the end, it would only hurt both of you."

But she could not blot out the image of him. Or the way she had felt when they had lain together, locked in each other's arms.

When morning came she got up and dressed and took her suitcase from the closet. Kumar had had her clothes brought from the house where she had lived for so short a time. Those were the only things she would take. The colorful caftans, the velvet slippers, the silky lingerie and the nighties she would leave behind.

She stayed in her room all that day. Tomorrow Kumar would leave, and though she longed to see him she would not. They had said all there was to say.

He spent most of the day with his father. Together they went over what had happened in the capital while Rashid had been gone, and discussed which of the men in the cabinet Rashid could trust.

The heads of the army and of the air force, as well as the captain of police were called in and together they went over plans and debated strategies on how best to repel an invasion from neighboring Azrou Jadida.

When finally the other men left, Rashid brought Kumar up-to-date on the warring desert tribes.

"Sheikh Ben Fatah is the one we have to worry about," he said. "He has many friends in Azrou Jadida and it would be in his best interests to sell our oil to them. Amin Elmusa is on the fence. He likes doing business with the United States and Europe, but offers of more money from Azrou Jadida have tempted him. He must be persuaded to fight with us. So must Sheikh Abdur Khan. He's a wily devil, so be careful of him.

"You'll be able to count on Jasmine's father. Youssef Abedi is a good man. You will stay with him while you're in the desert."

The discussion went on far into the afternoon. When at last Rashid pushed his chair back, he said, "I know that because you are a good Muslim you don't drink, Kumar. But if you did happen to have a drop of scotch, purely for medicinal purposes you understand, it would be most appreciated."

"That's the only reason I keep it, Father. Certainly I can see you're in need of something after such a long day. As I am."

He took a bottle out of one of the carved chests, and when he had poured an ample amount of the whiskey into two glasses, he handed one to Rashid.

"*Salam alekom,*" he said.

"And upon you, peace," Rashid responded.

They touched their glasses. "Tell me about the American woman," Rashid said.

Kumar set his glass on the table in front of him. "What would you like to know?"

"Are you sleeping with her?"

Kumar's mouth tightened. "No, I'm not."

"Why not?" Rashid swirled the whiskey around in his glass. "She's a beautiful woman, Kumar. I've seen the way the two of you look at each other and I know the attraction between you is strong. Why do you hesitate?"

"East doesn't always meet West, Father. Josie doesn't like Middle Eastern men."

"What?" Rashid looked startled. "What are you saying?"

"She worked in Il Hamaan for a while and hated it. I gather from what she's said that she was badly treated there. Also her best friend was married to a man from Jahan. The Jahanian brutalized her friend, and when they divorced he stole their son and took the child back to Jahan."

Kumar took a long swallow of his drink and in a voice filled with bitterness said, "She wants no part of me, Father. In her opinion all Middle Eastern men are alike."

Rashid's face darkened with anger. "It's up to you to show her otherwise. Tie her on a camel and take her into the desert with you. Make love to her six times a day and keep her there until she learns how to behave."

Kumar shook his head and with the barest suggestion of a smile said, "But don't you see that if I did what you suggest I would be confirming everything she thinks about us?"

"Maybe so," Rashid growled. "But that's exactly what your Bedouin grandfather would have done. He'd have taken her whether she wanted to go or not." He tapped Kumar's knee. "Remember, my son, you, too, are Bedouin."

"But I'm not my grandfather," Kumar said quietly. "Neither are you, Father. I know how gentle and kind you were to my mother, so don't tell me that you'd ever force yourself on a woman—because I know you would not."

"Maybe the American needs a little force to let her know what it is she really wants." He turned his piercing gaze on his son. "You're not in love with her, are you?"

It was a moment before Kumar answered. "No," he said, forcing a laugh. "I'm in lust. That's all."

But was it? He had lusted after women before, but surely he had felt for none of them what he felt for Josie. He wanted her, yes. But was there more to it than that? What was there about her that stirred his blood as no woman ever had?

It did no good to think of that now. It was over between them. Josie would go back to her own country and he would go into the desert with his people. They needed him. That's what mattered now.

When his father left, Kumar called for Saoud. "Tomorrow I leave for the desert," he said.

"I shall go with you, of course."

Kumar shook his head. "You'll join me later. I want you to stay here at the palace until Miss McCall leaves. When things calm down and it's safe to fly, you will see her safely onto my plane. Then you'll join me in the desert."

Saoud stroked his chin whiskers. "Why does she not accompany you? Have you asked her to?"

"Yes. She refused."

"Why do you not take her anyway? She is only a woman and you are a man. Once she is with you she will undoubtedly change her mind." He smiled. "About the desert, I mean."

Kumar's face went still. "You overstep," he said.

"And you will have me boiled in oil?" Saoud touched his fingertips to his forehead and bowed. "Very well," he said. "I will see to the American, and when she is safely out of Abdu Resaba I will join you in the desert. Is there anything else?"

"No, nothing."

"Then I shall take my most humble departure."

"You've never been humble a day in your life."

"Alas, that is true and will, I'm afraid, remain so." Saoud had been smiling, but now the smile faded. He put a hand on Kumar's shoulder. "Take care," he said. "These are dangerous times. Sharif Kadiri is an evil man and his tentacles reach far. There are men who would sell their own mothers for the money he would pay for your head. I should truly grieve if anything were to happen to you."

"Nothing's going to happen to me."

"I pray that is true. What time do you leave?"

"At dawn."

"May Allah protect you."

"And you, Saoud."

When he was alone Kumar hesitated, then crossed to the telephone. He had been angry when he'd left Josie the night before. He'd paced his rooms for hours after he'd left her, half tempted to go storming into her room and batter down the walls of her resistance.

She wanted him as badly as he wanted her. Why, then, had she stopped him? Were her prejudices so deeply ingrained she would not admit to herself what was between them?

Maybe his father was right. Maybe he should throw her on a camel and take her into the desert with him. He might be there for a month, maybe two. Two months with Josie. Two months of love-filled nights, of going to sleep with her beside him, waking in the night to rouse her to readiness. Of doing all the things with her he had ever dreamed of doing with a woman.

He swore aloud. Damn the woman! If she didn't want him, then let her take her prejudices and go back where she belonged. He'd be better off without her.

Maybe he'd say goodbye. Make it official. Final. He picked the phone up, held it for a moment, then put it down because he knew it would do no good to talk to her. It was better for both of them if they left things as they were.

But dear God, how he longed to see her just once more. To hold her again, to feel her softness, to breathe in the scent of her hair.

His hand tightened involuntarily on the phone, then with a curse he flung it across the room.

The next day he left for the desert.

It took two hours to reach the place where the caravan waited. When Kumar stepped out of the car in the dark gray *djellaba* with the black *ghutrah* covering his hair, some of the men he had known when he was in the desert before came forward to greet him.

"Sabbah al khair," they called out. "It is a morning of gladness to see you once more."

He greeted each of the eight men in turn and asked about their families. Their leader, a man whose name was Mohammed, said, "Everything is in order, Sheikh Kumar."

Sheikh Kumar? The name startled him. But that's how he would be known now that he was going into the desert. He smiled to himself because he knew how Josie would have reacted to his being called *sheikh*.

Josie. He must not think about her, for if he did he would turn the car around, race back to the palace, and do exactly what his grandfather would have done with such a woman. For a moment the temptation was so strong he had to clench his hands to his sides to keep from striding toward the car. To hell with her. He didn't need a woman who didn't want him the same way he wanted her. As soon as he reached the Bedouin camp he'd find a woman who would be only too glad to share his bed.

But in his heart Kumar knew that he would not. The only woman he wanted was Josie.

He turned to Mohammed. "If your men are ready, we'll leave immediately," he said.

"They are ready, Sheikh Kumar." Mohammed brought one of the camels forward and when he had whacked the beast across its knees with a stick and it had knelt, he said, "Let me help you."

"There's no need. I can manage. I . . ." He heard the sound of a motor. "What the devil?" he said, and saw a car racing toward them down the dusty road. When it drew closer he realized it was a limousine from the palace and he ran toward it, alarmed that something might have happened or that there had been a change in plans.

Before he could reach the car it stopped and Saoud got out. He opened the rear door and took out a canvas bag, then offered his hand to someone inside.

And Josie stepped out. She wore jeans and boots and a long-sleeved shirt. Her hair was pulled off her face in a braid. For a moment she didn't move, she only held on to Saoud's hand as if afraid to let go.

In a voice made rough by the shock of seeing her, Kumar said, "What are you doing here?"

Saoud let go of her hand. She took a step forward. "I wanted...I thought..." She swallowed hard, took a deep breath and said, "I want to go with you, Kumar. If you'll let me."

His heart started to race. Josie was here. She wanted to go with him. "The trip will be hard," he said. "It will take us three days to get to the Bedouin camp." He took a step toward her. "Why do you want to come with me?"

"You know why."

He felt his throat constrict. "Tell me."

She looked at the other men.

"They don't speak English. Tell me."

"I want to be with you."

"You know what will happen if you come."

"Yes, I know." Her gaze didn't falter. "I know."

"The Bedouin camp will be different from anything you've ever known."

"I understand."

"When we're there, we'll share a tent."

She nodded.

"And still you want to come with me."

"Yes," she said. "Oh, yes."

He let out the breath he didn't even know he'd been holding. He wasn't sure what miracle had brought her to him, he only knew that she was here and that she wanted to be with him.

He wanted to clasp her in his arms and tell her what this meant to him, but the other men were watching and so he led her to Mohammed and said, "This is Miss Josephine McCall from the United States. She and Saoud will accompany us."

The man touched his fingers to his forehead. *"Madame,"* he said. *"Marhaban,* welcome." He turned to

Saoud. "And to you, my tall friend. It is good to see you again."

"And you." Saoud glanced up at the sky. "It is daylight. We should be on our way before the sun is hot." He handed the canvas bag he had taken from the car to Mohammed. "These are the lady's things," he said.

Kumar took Josie's arm. "Have you ever ridden a camel?" he asked.

"No," she said. "But I'm a fairly good horsewoman."

"A camel is different."

"Oh?" She eyed the beast. He had a hairy drooping lip, yellow teeth and watery eyes.

Kumar helped her climb onto the saddle. "Hang on," he said, "and keep your feet back so that he doesn't bite you." He whacked the animal and it rose with a jolt that almost unseated her.

The camel huffed and groaned. It swung its neck around and the yellowed teeth reached for her ankle. Josie jerked her foot back and Mohammed struck the beast across his nose.

She clung to the saddle. "How long is the trip to where we're going?" she asked Kumar.

"Three days, if we're lucky. Four at the most."

Four days? On this droopy-lipped, yellow-fanged beast? With a sigh Josie settled herself into the saddle.

She still wasn't quite sure why she had decided to come. Perhaps it had been the dream of Kumar's riding into danger and the feeling that if she were with him she could somehow protect him. She'd known, too, that if she did not go with him it would be the end of things between them. The thought of that, of never seeing him again, had been insupportable. In time she would leave

him, but for now, for this time they would have together in the desert, she would be with him.

As for the trip, she'd been a camper since she was ten
years old and she'd won prizes for her horsemanship.
Surely this couldn't be so different.

An hour later she knew that it *was* different. For one
thing, horseback riding didn't make you seasick. She'd
heard that if you were on a ship and you kept your eyes
on something steady and straight the nausea would go
away. But how could you find something steady and
straight when with each rolling motion of the camel the
sand dunes rose and fell before your eyes?

By the time they stopped to rest, Kumar had to help
her off the camel.

"A queasy stomach?" he asked.

"Try total upheaval."

He walked her over to the shade of a date palm and
when Saoud had laid a piece of tarpaulin on the sand,
Kumar eased her down and held a canteen of water to
her lips. When she had taken a sip he said, "Take this
pill. It will help."

"Dramamine?"

"Something similar."

"You can't get seasick in the desert."

"A lot of people get sick the first time on a camel.
You'll feel better as soon as the pill takes effect."

"Wanna bet?"

He looked concerned. "We've only been gone an
hour," he said. "It's not too late to turn back. We'll wait
until the pill settles you down and then I can have Saoud
escort you."

"No." She put her hand on his arm. "I want to go
with you, Kumar. Don't send me back."

He brushed a tangle of hair back from her face. "What made you decide to come, Josie?"

"I'm not sure. Maybe it was something Jasmine said. Maybe it was a dream I had the night after you left me." She shook her head. "I couldn't leave things the way they were between us, Kumar. I want to be with you for this time in the desert. When it's over..." She tried to smile. "We'll talk about it then," she said. "In the meantime I want to be with you. All right?"

He took her hand and brought it to his lips. "It's more than all right, Josie. But we may be in the desert for a long time."

"I have time," she said.

When he left her she lay back on the tarp and closed her eyes. She slept and when she awoke her stomach had settled down. She drank some more water and she let Kumar wrap her head with a cloth to protect her from the sun. And when she was ready she climbed back on the camel.

By noon her body was drenched with sweat, but her stomach had settled and she was thankful for that. When they stopped for lunch, Saoud rigged a tarp over her head. She ate only a piece of flat bread and drank a glass of lime water. Her hands hurt from keeping such a tight hold on the reins, and her bottom was saddle sore.

Four days? she thought again.

All signs of civilization had been left behind. There was only mile after mile of endless sand and rolling dunes, broken occasionally by a few scrub plants or a cluster of date palms. Part of the time Kumar rode beside her. He looked different now than he had at the palace, all desert man in his flowing *djellaba* with the *ghutra* that covered his dark hair.

There were times during that long, hot afternoon when Josie asked herself what she was doing here in this strange and alien land with a man who was different from anyone she had ever known. Each time the doubts came she had only to look at Kumar to know the answer.

He had said that when they reached the Bedouin camp they would share a tent. She had known this was the way it would be and she didn't regret having come. She would stay with him for this time in the desert, and when it was over... No, she didn't have to think about that now. She would only think of the days—and the nights—that lay ahead.

And of how it would be when they reached the Bedouin camp.

When evening came they set up camp. After the tents were up the camel drivers started fires to prepare the evening meal.

Saoud brought Josie a basin of water and said, "I'm sorry. This is all that is allowed. I hope it will help."

And though she longed for a bath, Josie said, "Of course it will, Saoud. Thank you."

She took the binding off her head and unbraided her hair. She took off the shirt and bathed the best way she could. When that was done she brushed out her hair and put on a clean shirt from the bag she had brought with her.

Dinner consisted of dried meat with rice, hot nan bread, fruit and sugary mint tea. When she ate everything that was on her plate, Kumar smiled and said, "You have a good appetite. I like that in a woman."

She raised an eyebrow. "What else do you like in a woman, Prince Kumar?"

"Red hair," he said without hesitation. "Green eyes that I can get lost in. Smooth skin with just a sprinkling of freckles on the cheeks."

He leaned back on the sand, long legs stretched out in front of him, enjoying himself. "I prefer a woman who is tall," he went on. "A woman who stands eye to eye with me." His voice dropped to a seductive whisper. "I like a woman whose breasts are small enough for me to cup in the palm of my hand, whose nipples are the color of ripe peaches. I like a woman whose legs are long and shapely so that I can dream of how it will be when she puts them around my body. I like . . ."

He took a steady breath and his eyes blazed with a passion he could barely hold in check. "Do you know how much I want you?" he whispered. "Do you know what torture it is to say these things to you and not be able to take you in my arms because the men are watching us?"

She looked at him across the campfire that separated them. "I want to lie with you," she said, never taking her gaze from his. "I want to feel your body over mine. I want to make love with you." She took a deep breath. The tip of her tongue darted out to touch her upper lip. "I've wanted to for such a long time."

He ground his teeth together. "Why didn't you tell me?" he demanded hoarsely. "Why now, when there is nothing we can do about it?"

"Maybe that's why," she whispered with the hint of a smile.

Kumar didn't smile back. Holding her gaze, speaking in a voice so low she could barely hear, he said, "I've a good mind to grab you by the scruff of your neck and take you behind the nearest sand dune."

He got to his feet. His eyes were desert dark, his nostrils pinched with such barely restrained passion that for a moment she thought that was exactly what he was going to do. Instead he pulled her up beside him. His hands tightened on her arms and he kissed her.

"Our time will come," he said against her lips. "When it does, I'll make love to you until you plead for mercy. I'll kiss every inch of your body, and I'll make you wait until you beg me to take you."

Her knees went weak. She clung to him. "Kumar," she whispered. "Kumar."

He let her go. "Soon," he said. "Soon, my Josie."

On the morning of the fourth day they crested the top of a sand dune and saw below them the camp of Sheikh Youssef Abedi.

"We are here!" Mohammed called out.

A cry went up among the men. "*Yallah! Yallah!* Hurry!" Striking their camels to urge them on, they raced down the dune to the desert oasis.

Josie looked down on a city of black tents in an oasis of palm trees and spring-fed pools. There were fig and date palms, desert juniper, a sprinkling of flowers and small shrubs where goats and sheep grazed, and ground where wheat and barley grew.

Kumar reined in beside her. "This will be our home for the next few weeks," he said quietly. "I hope you will be happy here."

She turned on her saddle and looked into his eyes. "You will be with me. That's all that matters."

"Tonight you will lie in my arms. We will make love and afterward you will sleep in peace under my heart."

She reached out and touched his hand. And together they went slowly down the dune to the Bedouin camp that lay below.

Chapter 13

A crowd of men, women and children rushed out to greet them. Some of the women were veiled, some were not. Some had their heads covered, others had tattoos on their foreheads and cheeks, and most had henna on the palms of their hands. The younger girls wore dark skirts with brightly colored blouses; little boys wore either robes or white cotton pants and shirts.

All of them gathered around the new arrivals, shouting greetings at Kumar and the other men who had just arrived, pointing at the blue jeans Josie wore.

"Shoof!" they said. "Look! Look! The woman is wearing pants like a man. How is it possible?"

The men crowded closer. Most looked at her with anger and suspicion, but some with lust in their hooded eyes.

Josie clutched at the reins. For the first time since she had started out, she questioned the wisdom of coming. She hadn't expected to find a palace in the desert, but neither had she expected anything this primitive. It was too foreign, too different from anything she had ever known. It was as if she had stepped back into another time, another century.

She looked at Kumar for help, but before she could speak, one of the men cried out, "It is Sheikh Kumar Ben Ari!"

A cry went up and they pushed forward. "Sheikh Kumar! Sheikh Kumar! May Allah be praised."

Someone forced down his camel. He swung his legs over the saddle and they jostled each other to get closer to him.

He shouted greetings, clasped shoulders. These were his people and he was a part of them, all desert man now in his robe and *ghutra,* his skin darkened by the sun and his Bedouin ancestors.

The men pushed forward, surrounding Josie and the other riders in their eagerness to get closer. She looked to Kumar for help, but he was in the midst of them now, happy to be back, looking more at home here in this desert camp than he had been at the palace.

Suddenly over the cacophony of voices came one voice. The shouting stopped and the crowd, like the waves of the Red Sea, parted to make way for an old man.

He wore a robe so white it looked as if it had been bleached by a thousand days of sun. His face was lined, the bags beneath his eyes reddened by time. His ears stood out from his head like signal beacons able to pick up sounds one hundred miles away. His nose was large and veined, and his mustache dropped down over his full lower lip.

"Sheikh Abedi." Kumar bowed to the older man. "*Salam alekom,* my lord. Peace be upon you and upon your house."

"And upon you be peace, Sheikh Ben Ari. We are glad to have you with us once again. All that we have is yours and I bid you welcome."

"*Shukran.*" Kumar gestured to Saoud. "You know my friend?"

Youssef Abedi smiled. "Who could forget one such as he? You, too, are welcome, tall one."

"Thank you, my lord Abedi."

One of the camel tenders brought Josie's camel to its knees. Kumar helped her to dismount, and taking her hand, led her to Youssef Abedi.

"This is my woman," he said loudly enough for all of the others to hear.

"She is an American?" Abedi asked.

Kumar nodded. "She is a nurse with the International Health Organization. While we are here she will be happy to be of whatever service she can to the community. Perhaps tomorrow one of your women will teach her our ways."

With a nod, Abedi turned to a woman who had circled closer and motioned her forward. "This is Zaida. She will show you to the tent that has been prepared for you. Tomorrow she will instruct your woman on all she needs to know. Now you must rest, for you have had a long journey. Tomorrow we will talk." He touched his fingers to his forehead. "I'm glad you are here, Sheikh Kumar Ben Ari. Together, *inshallah,* we will unite the tribes."

"*Inshallah,* Sheikh Abedi."

The woman, Zaida, was middle-aged and skinny as a stick. She wore a faded blue robe. Her forehead was

tattooed in the design of a star, her hands were hennaed, and she had a gold earring in one nostril.

The men and women who had gathered around whispered among themselves as they stepped aside to let Kumar and Josie pass. But a small boy, braver than the rest,
ran up and tugged at Josie's hand.

"Why do you wear trousers?" he asked in a loud
voice. "Do you not know that it is *haram* for a woman
to wear trousers."

"I've been riding a camel for four days," she said. "It
was necessary."

"Will you wear the trousers now that you are here?"

Before she could answer, Zaida said, "Of course not,
Rafi. The lady will wear a robe like a proper woman."
She raised her hand. "Go before I box your ears."

He stuck out his tongue and darted off into the crowd.
"That boy," Zaida said with a shake of her head. "His
father should have him staked out over an anthill to
teach him some manners."

She led them past a long row of black tents to the far
side of the encampment. At last she paused, and indicating a tent that was larger than the others, motioned
for them to enter.

The sand floor was covered with Persian carpets,
scattered rugs and brightly colored tasseled pillows in
silk cases. There were hand-carved stools etched with
ivory and gold, a small table. In an open cabinet there
were silver cups and bowls and plates, water jugs,
gourds, and a teapot.

Colorful wool hangings hung from the sides of the
tent. There were chests for clothes and a low, wide sofa
with a blue silk spread.

It was primitive. It was colorful, and in its own way luxurious. Certainly it was different from anything Josie had ever seen.

Near the entrance of the tent there was a brazier, and pointing to it, Zaida said to Kumar, "Tomorrow I will teach your woman to cook for you."

"That would be appreciated."

"But tonight I will prepare your evening meal. Now I will bring water from the pond for you to bathe." She looked Josie up and down. "And a proper robe for *madame* to wear."

"Thank you, Zaida."

He saw the confusion in Josie's eyes, the uncertainty, and realized he had been so happy to be back, so busy saying hello to the men he knew and in greeting Sheikh Abedi, that he hadn't stopped to think how strange all of this must seem to her. If Bir Chagga had seemed different, this was another world.

She had been through four days of heat so hellish it would have had most men yelling for mercy. On the first day of the journey he'd had to help her off the camel and carry her to her tent because her legs had been shaking so badly from trying to stay on her beast that she couldn't walk. He had forced her to eat some bread and fruit and drink a cup of tea, but halfway through the meal she had fallen asleep.

The next morning she'd been so stiff she could barely walk. But she'd joked and said, "I guess you were right. A camel isn't anything at all like a horse."

That day and the following two days had not been easier. He'd called for a rest stop as often as he could, but never once had she asked him to. Never once had she complained.

Every one of those three nights in the desert he had sat by the fire looking at the tent where she slept, thinking of how it would be when they reached the Bedouin camp. But now that they were here, he thought ruefully, lovemaking would have to wait until she had rested.

When Zaida brought water, Kumar left the tent so that Josie could bathe and change. By the time he returned she was curled up on the sofa, fast asleep. He ate the dinner that Zaida prepared and when night fell he sat in front of the tent and smoked a cigarette.

The voices from the other tents were subdued. He heard a baby cry, a mother's soothing words and the laughter of children. A dog barked and a dozen others joined in. He could smell the cook pots, roasting goat meat and wheat cakes, cinnamon and coffee, rose water and camel dung.

This was his mother's land, these were her people and it was good to be back among them. For though he had gone to modern universities and had lived for a time in the western world, this was the place where he felt most at home. The desert was in his blood, for he was Bedouin.

Inside the tent a woman waited, a woman who could never be a part of his world. For this special time in the desert she would belong to him, but when their time ended she would go back to where she had come from.

He smoked another cigarette and when the moon was high he put it out and went in to her.

In the dim light of a lantern he saw that she had shifted onto her side. The white gown had slipped up over her hips, the silk sheet had slipped down.

He stood quietly for several minutes before he moved to the other side of the tent where he stripped out of his clothes and bathed. When he had finished he saw the clean robe Zaida had laid out for him, but he didn't put it on.

He blew out the light in the lantern and went back to the sofa and knelt beside the bed. He spoke her name, "Josie?" just once, and when she didn't answer he smiled and shook his head. As much as he wanted her he wouldn't disturb her. She was exhausted, he had to let her rest.

He lay down beside her and curled his naked body around hers. She murmured in her sleep but didn't awaken. He lifted the heavy hair off the back of her neck and kissed her there. "Sleep," he whispered. "When you awake it will be time enough for love to begin."

She dreamed that it was night and she was in a meadow, lying on her back in a field of wildflowers. The grass was soft under her back, so soft it was as if she were cradled in the earth.

A leaf of grass, or was it only the whisper of wind, gently stroked her breasts. She sighed and moved closer. The leaf of grass brushed her nipples as delicately as a lover's touch. Her body warmed. She yearned toward the touch.

"Josie?"

She opened her eyes, and by the light of the moon shining in through an opening in the top of the tent she saw him beside her.

"You were dreaming," he said.

"But I'm not dreaming now."

"No, love." He drew her into his arms and the whole length of him was naked against her.

For a moment she stiffened. In her half sleeping, half waking state, it seemed natural to awaken in his arms.

But she was awake now, a little frightened, a little unsure of herself.

"I've waited so long," he whispered.

"I . . . I know."

Kumar kissed her and a little of the tension eased. "So have I," she said.

He tightened his arms around her and the kiss deepened. When her body softened toward his, he touched her breasts through the fabric of her robe.

"Will you take it off for me?" he asked.

For the briefest fraction of a moment Josie hesitated. Then without a word she sat up and raised her arms over her head.

He took the gown away, and when she lay down beside him, he said, "I'm sorry it's dark. I want so badly to see you in the daylight with the sun on your body."

She kissed his shoulder and with a smile said, "Maybe you'd rather wait until daylight."

He shook his head. "I've already waited too long." He kissed her again and his body tightened with a terrible need, because he had wanted her for such a long time and because now she would be his.

He kissed her breasts, slowly, tenderly. He took one poised and hardened peak between his teeth and held it there to lap and tease.

She dug her fingers into his shoulders and her body burned with such pleasure she did not think she could stand it. But when he made as though to move away, she said, "Oh, don't. Not yet."

It was torture to wait, but how he loved her responding to him like this. He touched both breasts, one with his mouth and the other with his fingers, until her body arched to his and she cried, "Oh, please. Oh, please, Kumar, I can't bear it."

"Say my name again," he whispered against her flesh.

"Kumar." She pulled his head up and brought his mouth to hers. "Kumar," she whispered against his lips. "Kumar."

"Tell me . . ."

"Anything."

"Tell me you want me."

"Oh, yes. Oh, yes. I want you."

He came over her. She felt his quivering hardness against her thigh and her body jerked with reaction.

He parted her legs with his knee. He kissed her mouth, he rained kisses over her face, her ears, her throat. He kissed each breast again and again, and when she began to tremble he raised himself above her. Grasping her hips he whispered her name in a hush of passion . . . "Shozee" . . . and joined his body to hers.

He thrust so hard and deep it took away her breath. She couldn't speak. It took everything she had not to cry out with the sheer pleasure of having him inside her.

He moved like a man possessed and his breath came in painful gasps. He grasped her hands and entwined her fingers with his. She clasped him with her legs and he whispered, "I've dreamed of you doing this. Dreamed . . ."

His mouth crushed hers and his tongue was silky hot inside her mouth, plunging as his body plunged. He gave no respite, nor did she ask for one. His cadence quickened. He let go of her hands and she put her arms around him and held him as he held her. She lifted her body to his and whispered his name in the darkness of the night.

He slid his hands beneath her and rocked her closer, so close that she became a part of him, bone of his bone and flesh of his flesh. She arched her body against his and knew she was losing control. This was... Oh, sweet heaven. It was too much. It was everything.

She couldn't think, could only feel this frenzied passion that was part agony, part ecstasy. Covered by the moonlight, by him, she lifted her body to his and wept with a completion that shattered her very soul and rendered her helpless in his arms.

He took her mouth. His body arched above her. His eyes narrowed and with his head thrown back he thrust deep and hard. Again and again before, with an agonized cry of "Josie! Josie!" he collapsed over her.

They held each other, hearts beating hard, pulses racing.

"I knew..." He had to gasp for air. "I knew from the first moment I saw you it would be like this." He kissed the side of her face and felt her tears. "Why do you weep?" he asked. "Did I hurt you? Did I—?"

She stopped his words with a kiss. "No, of course you didn't hurt me. It's just..." She shook her head. "It was so much. So incredibly much, Kumar."

"As it should be." He drew her back into his arms. "Now we will sleep close, like this, yes? And perhaps when we awake we will make love again."

She ran her fingertips across his lips. "Perhaps," she said.

He slept a deep and dreamless sleep. In the first light of dawn, in that stage between sleeping and waking, he felt her hand upon him. Her fingers were warm, gentle, and he grew hard in her hand. And though he smothered a moan, he didn't open his eyes, but lay still, pretending to sleep, letting her minister to him.

Last night he had been afraid he wouldn't please her, that she wouldn't respond with the passion he had hoped for. He had known it would be good, but he hadn't expected spectacular.

He had told himself that if it was not as good the first time, as often happened with a woman, it would be better the next time.

He didn't think it could get any better. Skyrockets had gone off in his head. He'd felt as if he'd received ten thousand volts of electricity, all directed at that most virile part of him. He'd never felt that way before, had never experienced with any other woman what he had experienced with Josie that night.

Still holding him, she leaned to kiss his mouth.

He ran his tongue across her lips. "You taste so good," he whispered.

"You feel so good," she said.

He opened his eyes and smiled at her. "You know you're driving me crazy, don't you?"

"I hope I am."

He ran his hand down the length of her back, then gentled her over. While she still touched him, he slid his hand between her legs and stroked the warmth and moistness there.

"So soft," he murmured. "So ready."

She turned her head into his shoulder. "Kumar," she said. "Oh, darling."

The word was like a caress against his skin and he knew he couldn't wait. Quickly, so quickly he heard the whispered "whoof" of her breath, he rolled her beneath him and pressed his body to hers. She put her arms around him and held him close. He kissed her and her lips parted under his. He rubbed his body against hers and she lifted herself to him.

He said, "Open your legs to me," and she opened them.

He raised himself over her. Her eyes really are the color of the Nile, he thought. She is so beautiful she takes my breath away.

He eased that throbbing part of him between her legs, rubbed it against her until he was near to bursting, then with a low cry thrust into her.

She held him with her arms and with her legs. She said, "Oh, yes. Oh, Kumar, Kumar."

He took her mouth and kissed her with all of the passion of his pent-up body. He moved deep inside her. Her warmth closed in about him and he knew this was the closest he would ever be to heaven.

He moved slowly, deeply, luxuriating in the feel of her. He bent to kiss her breast. He caught her nipple between his teeth and lapped the peaked and ready nub. She writhed against him and lifted her body to his. She met his every thrust and whispered of her pleasure.

"Slowly, *laeela,*" he whispered. "Wait, love. Make it last, love."

She tried, but oh, it was difficult. He moved against her with such exquisite slowness, his body shaking with what it cost him to wait. But soon, too soon, his breath came in shuddering gasps and though he tried to hold back he could not. He plunged and withdrew, plunged and withdrew. And when she cried, "I can't bear it. I can't..." and her body moved like a wild thing under his, he gripped her hands and lifting them above her head, he cried, "Look at me. Look at me when it happens."

She opened her eyes and her pupils were dilated with sexual excitement.

He plunged once more and she cried out as if she had been mortally wounded. She lifted herself to him, struggling against the hands that held her, and when he let her go she clasped him closer.

"Josie!" he gasped. "Josie!" And with one violent thrust, his body shook in a paroxysm of pleasure that left him spent and weak against her.

They couldn't speak. They kissed each other's faces, throats, shoulders. He stroked her back, she threaded her fingers through his hair. When at last he rolled away from her he reached for her hand, and bringing it to his lips he kissed each fingertip.

There was so much he wanted to say, so many things he could not say. He was shocked by the immensity of what he felt for her.

He had wanted her since that night in California after the wedding rehearsal. He had promised himself then that some day he would have her, and had told himself that once he'd had his fill of her he would be able to turn and walk away.

He knew now that just the opposite might be true, that the more he had of her the more he would want.

That wasn't the way he had planned it.

He sat up and moved away from her. "Sleep if you can. I have to see Sheikh Abedi."

"You're leaving me at the mercy of Zaida?"

"You'll be in good hands. Perhaps in time she'll make a proper desert woman out of you." He grinned down at her. "Have you ever milked a camel?"

A look of sheer horror crossed her face. "Milked...a camel?"

"Strengthens the fingers," he said with a wicked gleam in his eye. Then, because he was afraid if he didn't leave he'd want to make love with her again, he got up. "I'll be busy most of the day. Look around the camp if you'd like to. I'll see you later."

She watched him walk across the tent. His shoulders were wide. His stomach was flat, his hips were narrow, his legs were straight and strong and long. And he had great buns.

She pulled the blue sheet up to her chin and smiled, glad now that she had come, even if it did mean she'd have to milk a camel.

Chapter 14

The following morning Kumar met with Youssef Abedi to discuss the situation in Bir Chagga and the possibility of uniting the desert tribes.

Abedi confirmed what Rashid had told Kumar about the sheikhs of the ruling Bedouin tribes. "Amin Elmusa is undecided," he said. "But I have a feeling he will be the easiest to convince. As for Abdur Khan..." Youssef tugged on his earlobe. "We must go cautiously. He will go to whatever side will be most beneficial to him. It doesn't matter that Abdu Resaba is his country, he will sell his oil to the highest bidder and side with whoever he thinks has the best chance of winning the war."

"And what of Nasir Ben Fatah?" Kumar asked.

"That son of a camel!" Youssef's face hardened. "He would sell his soul to the devil if he thought it would bring a profit. He's done business with Azrou Jadida in the past, and he will again if the price is right. If war comes you can count on the fact that he will side with whoever offers him the most."

"I'll talk to him."

"It will do no good."

"Nevertheless, I must try. When can we see him?"

Youssef tugged on his other earlobe. "First we should talk to the other two, Amin Elmusa and Abdur Khan. Their camps are no more than five miles apart and roughly twenty miles from here. Perhaps if we can tell Ben Fatah we have them on our side, he will capitulate. If we ride out at dawn tomorrow we should reach Elmusa's camp by late afternoon. I'll send a messenger ahead to say that we're coming."

He offered a hookah to Kumar and when Kumar shook his head, Youssef lighted the water pipe, and after he had puffed for a few minutes in silence, said, "We'll spend the night with Elmusa and the next day we'll see Sheikh Khan. After that it will take us another day to reach Ben Fatah's camp."

He lay back on the pillows and puffed on the pipe for several minutes before he said, "It could be dangerous. Ben Fatah has no love for your father, nor for you. I am thinking that perhaps after we leave Khan you should return here and let me go on alone to see Ben Fatah."

"Absolutely not. I have no intention of letting you take a risk while I ride for safety. We go to the camp of Ben Fatah together."

"As you wish, Kumar. But every second we are there you must watch him the way the snake charmer watches the cobra. Do not turn your back on him lest you end up facedown on the sand with a dagger in your back."

Once again Sheikh Abedi drew in on his pipe. "Tell me what the situation is in Bir Chagga."

"Things are quiet at the moment, but there's the smell of danger in the air. There haven't been any more demonstrations or riots, which seems to confirm the fact that Sharif Kadiri was behind them."

"I met him once, years ago. He talked of insurrection even then. I know he's a good military strategist, but I never understood why your father wanted him in his cabinet."

"It was a mistake."

"A costly one. Kadiri and Ben Fatah are birds of a feather, vultures who care nothing about their homeland. If they are in this together, coconspirators who will fight with Azrou Jadida, then we will need all of the men we can get to fight against them."

"If all goes well on our trip we will have them."

Youssef puffed hard on his pipe. "There is something I should tell you, Kumar Ben Ari. I have heard rumors that Kadiri has a price on your head. He knows that soon your father will step down and that once he does you will rule Abdu Resaba. His thinking is that with you out of the way he can march on Bir Chagga and become the head of the country."

"He's mistaken," Kumar said angrily. "Even if something should happen to me, my father will continue to rule Abdu Resaba as he always has. My father is a good man, Youssef. He'd never let Abdu Resaba fall into the hands of a man like Sharif Kadiri."

"*Inshallah.*" Youssef leaned farther back into his pillows. "I have known your father for many years, Kumar. He is my friend and I know what you say is true." He puffed on the water pipe and a smile softened his features. "I was with him the day he met your mother. He had come from Bir Chagga on a caravan trip. He and the men he was with had planned to stop here for only a day or two before they went on.

"The night he arrived he met your mother. She was veiled of course, but even veiled it was possible to tell that Zenobia was beautiful. She was seventeen and he was twenty-four. I think he fell in love with her that first night. He didn't leave as he had planned. At the end of the first week he asked Zenobia's father for her hand in marriage and when her father gave his consent, Rashid asked, though it wasn't the custom, that she, too, give her consent.

"They were married three days later, and when he returned to Bir Chagga, she went with him."

Youssef looked at Kumar and his red-lidded eyes were serious. "You see, even though your mother was a Bedouin and your father was not, they were of the same faith, the same Arabic blood. That is as it should be, as it must be. It is not right that our blood mix with the blood of the infidels. Remember that, my boy."

"You speak of my woman," Kumar said, trying to hold back the anger from his voice.

Youssef nodded. "She's very beautiful. I can understand your interest in her, but you must remember that she is not one of us. Enjoy her while you are here in the desert, but know that when you leave it must end."

He had told himself exactly that, but the words were hard when they came from the lips of Youssef Abedi. Because he could not speak of her to Youssef, Kumar rose.

"I'll take my leave of you now, sir," he said, "so that I can prepare for our departure tomorrow."

"If I have offended you, I'm sorry."

"You have not offended." Kumar paused at the opening of the tent. "Until tomorrow," he said.

He didn't go back to his own tent, but went instead to the edge of camp where he could be alone with his thoughts. The old man was right, of course. When the time came for him to take Josie back to Bir Chagga, it would be the end of their relationship. That's the way it had to be.

And yet...

Last night with her had been more than he had dreamed lovemaking could be. For a long time he had lain with his naked body pressed to hers, and when he could stand it no longer he had awakened her. She had come willingly into his arms, all warmth and softness and sweet scents. And when he had joined his body to hers she had met his passion in a way that had taken his breath.

Afterward, when they lay spent in each other's arms, it had been like coming home, like finding shelter after a storm. It had been so much more than sexual release, it had been like finding another part of himself.

He returned to their tent to find her taking a bath in a round tin tub.

"Isn't this wonderful?" she said when he pulled back the curtain that hid her from view. "Zaida brought it in this morning after you left. A little while ago she and I filled it with buckets of water from the pond."

Kumar didn't speak, he only looked at her.

"What is it?" she asked. "Is something wrong?"

"No." He knelt beside the tub and took the washcloth from her.

"Kumar...?"

"Shh. Let me do this for you." He soaped her shoulders, her back and her breasts. He lingered over the tender peaks, rubbing and teasing them between his fingers. He drew the soap bubbles out to a point and leaning close blew them away.

"Darling?" Her voice was husky. "Oh, darling."

That word. That one word. Darling. It made him feel like a king. Like a man.

"Lie back," he said. And when she did he touched between her legs, first with the cloth, then with his hands.

Her eyes drifted closed; he could feel her tremble.

The water was cool, but she was warm. Soapy soft as he stroked his fingers round and round the triangle of curls. Round and round her heated core, and glided a finger so easily inside. Circling, circling.

"Oh, please," she whispered. "Please."

He took her hand and helped her out of the tub. He dried her, and when he finished he knelt before her and leaned his head against her belly.

She touched the top of his head. Her legs were trembling.

He brought her closer and kissed her in that most special of places, kissed her with his lips and his tongue. Kissed her until her legs began to tremble and she had to cling to him for support.

When it became too much she struggled against the hands that held her, but he wouldn't let her go. Though she cried out he cradled her until with a smothered scream her body stiffened and shook with a passion that left her helpless in his arms.

Before she could recover he laid her on the Persian carpet and with a cry of need plunged hard into her. It was fast, it was fierce, and when it was over she clung to him, too spent to speak.

He stroked her to calmness. And tried not to think of how it would be when the time came to let her go.

* * *

They left before dawn. Kumar, Sheikh Youssef and Saoud, along with a retinue of twenty of Youssef's best men.

The air was refreshingly cool and Kumar felt invigorated, full of life and health. He loved the desert and the feel of a fine horse under him. But that was only part of it, of course. The other part was Josie and the way she made him feel.

This morning, in the dim light of the lantern, he had looked down at her. She had been asleep, her hair spread like a fan over the pillow, one soft roundness of breast exposed, one bare leg stuck out from the sheet. And though they had made love only an hour before he had wanted her again.

No woman had ever affected him the way Josie did. No woman had ever roused this kind of need in him. He wasn't sure he liked her having this much power over him. It was something he needed to think about.

Sheikh Amin Elmusa was a small, skinny man, who looked as though he hadn't the strength to climb onto a camel. But looks were deceiving; he had four wives and twenty-three children.

He welcomed Youssef and Kumar into his tent with much bowing and scraping and ordered one of his wives to serve their tea. The woman, when she came, was at least twenty years younger than Amin and obviously quite pregnant.

With a proud smile he patted her belly. "This one will be number twenty-four," he said.

They drank their tea and he asked about the situation in Bir Chagga.

"It's quiet at the moment, but there will be a war," Kumar said. "I've come here to unite the desert tribes into a fighting force, so that when the time comes we will march on the city as one unit." He hitched forward on his pillow. "How many men do you have, Sheikh Amin?"

"Almost a thousand."

"Good," Kumar said with a nod. "My father has been your trusted friend for many years. Now he is asking for your help." He took a sip of the hot, sweet tea. "The United States has been a friend to us and we want to continue supplying them with oil."

"Azrou Jadida also wants our oil. They will pay more than the United States."

"For how long?" Kumar asked. "They're a small country, and warlike. Who knows what will happen there next year or the year after that? The United States will continue to buy your oil year after year. Why take a chance on a few extra dollars for a short time, when you can be assured millions of dollars for years to come?"

Amin stroked his thinning chin whiskers. "There is something in what you say, Sheikh Ben Ari. I will think about it and in a week's time you will have my answer."

Two of his other wives served them. Both of them were in varying stages of pregnancy. When they had finished eating, wife number four appeared to serve their coffee. She, too, was with child.

"No wonder he is skin and bones," Youssef said when he and Kumar were alone. "He's so busy keeping his women pregnant I doubt that he'll have time to fight with us."

"Even if he doesn't, he'll order his men to fight. I think we can count on him, Youssef, and if we can convince Sheikh Khan when we see him tomorrow, we'll have a fighting force of almost three thousand."

"With my men you will have another thousand," Youssef said.

"And if Ben Fatah joins us we'll have at least five."

"Do not count on Ben Fatah," Youssef said. "As for Abdur Khan . . . Well, tomorrow we shall see."

Khan was, as Kumar's father had told him, as wily as a fox. He advanced, he retreated. One moment he seemed about to accede to their wishes, the next moment he hesitated.

He fed them well and that night he entertained them with dancing girls.

But he refused to say whether he would or would not join them in their fight.

The following morning they left for the camp of Sheikh Nasir Ben Fatah.

Ben Fatah was six feet tall. His shoulders were broad, his stomach was round. In his black-and-white striped robe, he was a massive figure. His eyes were as small and black as a raven's. The three-day growth of beard did not hide the deep lines that ran from his nose to his mouth. He wore a belt around his black-and-white striped robe. There was a jewel-handled dagger in the scabbard that was strapped to his waist.

"*Marhaban,*" he said when they rode into his camp. "Welcome to my home, Sheikh Abedi. And you, Sheikh Kumar Ben Ari. Come, let us go into my tent. You've had a long journey and I'm sure you're tired. I've had a small repast prepared, which my women will bring when you are ready."

He motioned Youssef and Kumar ahead, but stopped with a frown when he saw that Saoud intended to accompany them. "Your man will be served outside," he told Kumar.

"I go where my lord Kumar goes," Saoud said.

"It's his habit." Kumar shrugged and a slight smile tugged at the corners of his mouth. "He thinks of himself as my protector, and there's little I can do about it."

"I'd do something about it," Ben Fatah answered with a growl. "I'd have him tied to a post and lashed for his insolence."

Saoud didn't speak, but there was a flash of anger in his eyes that made Ben Fatah say, "Yes, yes. Very well. But he is a servant and will sit apart from us."

They entered the tent. It was large and unkempt. Stained rugs covered the sand, floor pillows were scattered about. There were camel saddles, a bed with rumpled bed covers, a low table.

Ben Fatah motioned them to sit before he clapped his hands and shouted, "Women! Serve us now."

The three men sat cross-legged in front of the table. Saoud sat behind Kumar. Three robed women came in. Their eyes behind their veils looked frightened. The food looked unappetizing.

And it was. The lamb was greasy, the couscous was cold, the chicken tough. Ben Fatah ate with his fingers, and licked each one with a loud, sucking sound after every bite.

When at last the food had been taken away and the too-sweet mint tea had been served, Ben Fatah said, "Now, shall we get to the reason for your visit?"

"My reason is a simple one." Kumar wiped his hands on the cloth that had been provided. "Abdu Resaba is on the verge of a civil war. A former minister of my father's, Sharif Kadiri, has turned traitor. We're sure that he's in Azrou Jadida raising men to fight against us."

"It is a question of oil, of course." Ben Fatah wiped the grease from his mouth with the back of his hand. "Oil and money, yes?"

Kumar nodded. "I've come to the desert to try to convince the tribes that we must unite because the welfare of our country is at stake. We must stand as one united nation against Azrou Jadida."

"I've done business with Azrou Jadida from time to time and have had no trouble with them."

"Oil business." Kumar frowned. "I know that. And you know that for many years our country has had an agreement to sell oil to the European countries as well as to the United States. Azrou Jadida will use the oil you would sell them to make war on smaller, more defenseless countries."

"That's no concern of mine."

Kumar, trying to hold on to his temper, leaned forward. "They would make war on our country," he said.

Ben Fatah took a sip of his tea. "I'm Bedouin. The desert is my home."

"But you are a citizen of Abdu Resaba," Youssef protested. "You can't turn your back on your country."

"I can do anything I want to do, if the money is right." All pretense at cordiality vanished. "If there is a war, Sharif Kadiri will win. And when he does, if I have sold my oil to Azrou Jadida as he has asked me to, I'll be the richest man in the desert."

He stood and with a hand on the sheathed dagger said, "Go back to your father and tell him that it is I, Nasir Ben Fatah, who rules the desert. Not him, not you.

Tell him that I will sell my oil to whomever I please. If war comes I ride with Sharif Kadiri.''

He took a step toward Kumar. "I do favors for my friends," he said in a low and threatening voice. "Kadiri is my friend. You, the whoreson of that bastard Rashid, are not.''

Kumar jumped to his feet. But Ben Fatah had the advantage. He reached for the jeweled dagger, yanked it out of its scabbard and lunged at Kumar. The knife slashed out. Kumar threw himself to one side. The knife missed his chest but slashed his arm. He cried out and reached for his gun. Before he could get it, Saoud jumped forward and brought the edge of his hand down on Ben Fatah's wrist. Ben Fatah swore; the dagger fell to the sand.

Youssef gripped Kumar's arm. "You're hurt!" he cried.

Kumar shrugged him away and started toward Ben Fatah.

The other man's face was livid with rage. "Abdulah!" he called out. "Faouzi!"

Two men, guns drawn, rushed in. Saoud grabbed Ben Fatah around his neck and held the dagger to his throat.

"We will leave as we came." Kumar clutched his bloody arm. "Warn your men not to attack us from behind. If they do, Nasir Ben Fatah, be assured you will be the first to fall.''

The three of them, with Saoud holding Ben Fatah in front of him, strode out of the tent. A dozen of Ben Fatah's men were waiting for them. In back of them, surrounding them, were Youssef's men.

"Don't shoot!" Ben Fatah screamed.

His men stepped back.

Kumar, Youssef and Saoud, holding Ben Fatah in front of him, elbowed their way past the armed men. Saoud hoisted Ben Fatah onto his horse, got on behind him, and held the other man's dagger to his throat.

Ben Fatah's men backed away. The three men, with Youssef's twenty men bringing up the rear, rode out of the camp. Half a mile later they stopped and Saoud let Ben Fatah slide down to the sand.

"Go home," Kumar said.

Ben Fatah glared up at him and raised his fist. "I promise that you will regret this day."

Kumar stared down at the man who had tried to kill him. And knew that before this was over one of them would fall.

Chapter 15

During the five days that Kumar was away from the camp Josie learned to milk not a camel but a goat.

The first time she tried, the other women whispered behind their hennaed hands. But when they saw that she was willing to learn, they offered advice and one or two of them came forward to help her.

When the early morning milking was done the women went to work in the section of land where they grew barley and millet, wheat, lentils and broad beans. It was a surprise to Josie that here in the desert there was enough fresh water from the springs to irrigate the land. But there was, and food was no problem. In addition to what they raised, there were date palms and fig trees, as well as goats and camels for milk, and sheep for shish kebab.

The Bedouins were a healthy, hearty people. Because the tribe was considered to be one large family, the women weren't veiled. They were friendly and talk-tive, more open with each other than women from the city.

In the evening before dinner they went in groups to different sections of the desert pools to bathe. There, hidden by the trees, they removed their undergarments from under their robes, and still wearing their robes, waded into the water.

This was the time when the heat of the day had ebbed, the time to gossip and laugh, to speak about their families and their friends.

Little by little they came to accept Josie, as she came to accept them. Although she would have preferred to bathe without the cumbersome robe, she did as they did. Her language skills had improved during this time in the desert and she was able to understand the jokes they made, the stories they told.

They asked questions about where she had come from and why she was here in the desert with Sheikh Kumar.

"Are you to marry?" Zaida asked one evening.

Marry? That gave her pause. The word marriage had never been mentioned, perhaps, she thought now, because both she and Kumar knew that it was impossible. He was Muslim, she was Christian. The saying that East is East and West is West and never the twain shall meet was true. And though she loved him . . . She took a deep breath because even thinking about the *L* word frightened her.

She wasn't sure when she had fallen in love with Kumar, but she had. Perhaps it had happened that very first day when she had stepped off the plane and seen him there waiting for her, wearing his desert robe, looking up at her with his dark desert eyes.

Perhaps it had been when they kissed in that small and intimate alcove at the residence he had provided for her.

Or the day of the riot when he had covered her bod
with his.

All that mattered was that she *had* fallen in love, an
that she didn't know what to do about it.

"Will you have children?" another woman ques
tioned.

She looked at the woman, for a moment too stunne
to speak. Had that even crossed her mind? During an
of those nights she and Kumar had lain together had sh
even once given thought to the consequences?

She was a nurse, a trained medical professional wh
spoke to women in third-world countries about birth
control. Yet she had taken no precautions when she ha
come into the desert with Kumar.

There hadn't been any reason to buy birth-control pill
when she'd first come to Abdu Resaba, because makin
love with Kumar Ben Ari had been the farthest thing
from her mind. When she had decided to come into the
desert with him there had been no time to do anything
about it. For the past few days she'd been playing Rus
sian roulette, she might already be pregnant.

She wasn't sure how she felt about that. If she wer
carrying his child . . .

The women looked at her, curious, questioning.

She lifted her shoulders in an I-don't-know gesture
and they smiled.

But under cover of the water she slipped her hand un
der her robe and rested it over her naked stomach. Wa
she pregnant? And if she was, how did she feel about it'
Scared? Yes, a little. Pleased? Maybe. No, not maybe
Yes. *Yes.* For if it were true that she was pregnant with
Kumar's child, she would take a part of him with he
when she left this place. It would be a part of him sh
would always have.

* * *

Kumar's wound, though not serious, had weakened him. And though he protested, the others stopped often to let him rest.

"We should press on," he insisted each time they did. "What if Ben Fatah's men come after us? We're only twenty-three against hundreds. We have to keep moving."

"If we do you will bleed to death," Saoud said.

"Saoud is right." Youssef looked out at the desert dunes that rose and fell in a heat so intense it took their breaths. "Ben Fatah won't attack during the day," he said. "He is like the jackal that sneaks around in the dark. If he attacks it will be at night."

And though Kumar insisted that they push on, they made their way slowly, resting from the sun at midday, traveling until it was too dark to see. So it was that three days passed before they reached the crest of the dune that looked down on Youssef's camp.

It was dusk when a shout rang out that they had been seen. By the time they made their way down the dune, the men who had been left behind hurried out to greet them. As did the women returning from their evening bath.

"Your man is back," Zaida called out to Josie.

"Kumar?" She dropped what she was doing and ran toward the advancing men.

Kumar saw her. He lifted his arm in a salute. Then his body drooped and as if in slow motion he leaned forward and slipped from the saddle.

Two men caught him before he fell and eased him down to the sand.

"What is it?" Frantic with fear, Josie pushed her way through the crowd of men. "Let me through!" she cried.

Saoud, who had jumped from his saddle before his camel had time to kneel, ran to Kumar. "It's a knife wound," he said to Josie. "It happened four days ago. He's lost a lot of blood.

Fear gripped her and for a moment she was almost too terrified to move. Kumar was unconscious. His face was pale. The bandage on his arm was soaked with blood. Kumar! Dear God, if anything happened to him...

She knelt on the sand and felt for his pulse. It was irregular. His skin was heated. From the sun or a fever? She wasn't sure.

"Take him to our tent," she said to the men gathered around.

Two of them stepped forward, but before they could lift him Saoud pushed them aside, and bending down gathered Kumar in his arms.

"Bring boiling water," Josie told Zaida. "Alcohol, a clean white cloth for a bandage. Hurry!"

When they reached the tent, Josie and Saoud took off Kumar's dusty robe and she removed the bandage from his arm. The cut was deep and jagged, but it had closed. And though it was crusted with dried blood there seemed to be no sign of infection.

"I made a poultice from a yucca plant," Saoud said. "I hope it helped."

"It did." They eased him back on the bed. "What happened?" Josie asked.

"We were in the camp of Ben Fatah. There was an argument. The son of a serpent did it before I could get to him. If Kumar hadn't reacted as quickly as he did, the knife would have reached his chest." He bowed his head. "It's my fault he was wounded. If I had been quicker—"

"No, Saoud. You brought him back, that's what matters. He's here and he's alive. Now it's up to me to make him well again." Josie put a hand on his arm. "And I will, Saoud. I promise you, I will."

Zaida and another woman came in with the things Josie had asked for. She wet a piece of cloth with the alcohol and held it under Kumar's nose. He coughed and she said, "Kumar? It's Josie. You're here now, Kumar. You're safe."

"Josie?"

"Yes, darling." She smoothed the hair back off his forehead. "I'm going to clean the wound, Kumar. I'm afraid it will hurt, but it has to be done. I'm sorry."

He nodded. "Go ahead."

She bathed his arm with soap and water, then with alcohol. He winced and closed his eyes.

"Just the bandage now," she said, and taking the clean strips of cloth from Zaida, she bandaged the wound.

He opened his eyes. *"Shukran,"* he murmured. Then, "Tired. Need to sleep."

"In a few minutes, Kumar. I need to bathe you."

She washed him with soap and cool water. His skin was still hot when she finished, so she poured some of the alcohol into a bowl and bathed him with that.

"Feels good," he mumbled. "Cool."

"Yes, Kumar. You'll feel better now."

Zaida brought soup. Saoud raised Kumar's shoulders and Josie spooned the hot broth into his mouth. He finished half of it before he shook his head and said, "No more."

Saoud eased him back down on the bed. "I will be just outside the tent," he told Josie. "If you need anything you have but to call."

When they were alone, Kumar took her hand. "Come lie with me," he said.

Josie took off her sandals and came in beside him. He put his good arm around her. "Don't leave me," he whispered.

"I won't."

He closed his eyes. His breathing evened and he slept.

She looked at him. There were dark smudges caused by pain and fatigue under his eyes, and lines around his mouth that hadn't been there before. But he was safe and he was here.

Tears stung her eyes and she made no effort to hold them back. If anything had happened to him... The thought, like a knife as sharp as the one that had wounded him, sliced through her. She wept silently, with relief that the wound had not been more serious, and because she loved him.

He moaned in his sleep. "I'm here," she whispered and kissed his shoulder. "I'm here, Kumar, for as long as you want me to be."

Three days later he was strong enough to walk around the camp. He ate well and slept each night with Josie beside him.

Near the end of the week a rider came with word from Amin Elmusa.

"My men will ride with you," the note Amin had sent read. "You tell us when. We are ready. We will fight beside you."

The following day Abdur Khan rode in with ten of his men. "I have thought carefully of what you told me," he said to Kumar when they met in Youssef's tent. "I believe it's to my best interests to be with you and your father. When the trouble comes I will be at your side."

The trouble was surely coming. Word arrived from his father that troops were gathering at the border between Azrou Jadida and Abdu Resaba.

"We know they will strike," his father wrote. "The army and the air force are on the alert, but we need the Bedouins. What news do you have? Will they be with us? Can we count on them?"

Kumar wrote back:

Elmusa and Khan are with us. With them and with Youssef we will have more than four thousand men. I can promise you a strong fighting force that I will lead to Bir Chagga.

He began to train Youssef's men. They were all good riflemen, of course, and needed only to be better organized to fight as one strong and united group. Kumar spent the major part of the day with them, but the rest of the time he spent with Josie.

She had changed during her time in the desert. She looked tanned and fit as she strode through the camp in her robe and sandals, her hair in a braid down her back, greeting both men and women as though they were old friends.

The first morning she moved out of his arms and said, "I have to get up, I have milking to do," he looked at her as though she'd lost her mind.

"Milking?" he asked, dumbstruck.

"Goats." She grinned. "Actually, I'm quite good at it."

He let her go and later he walked down to where the women were and saw her milking. Dressed in her robe, kneeling on the sand beside the goat, with her head against his belly, she looked no different than the other women who knelt to do their milking.

Where had the woman who had been Josie McCall gone? he wondered. What had happened to that smartly dressed woman who wore her hair pulled back off her face in an elegant chignon, who dressed in a silk suit and high heels? What had become of her?

He thought of his father then, and wondered if this was how Rashid had felt when he'd come to this same camp so many years ago and seen the woman who was to be his wife.

Had he felt this same surge of tenderness? This same heart-stopping desire? This love.

But love was something Kumar didn't want to think about.

This was the here and the now, this time in the desert with Josie. It was enough. It was everything. He would not think beyond this.

Each evening when he returned to their tent he started a fire in the brazier, so that she could cook their evening meal.

She wasn't a good cook. She made a mess of the wheat cakes. She burned the shish kebab, and her hummus— the chickpeas cooked with lemon juice and garlic— looked like leftover cat food.

He didn't complain. He ate whatever she prepared and tried to fill up on flat bread. So he'd lose a few pounds, fade away like Amin Elmusa to skin and bones. It didn't matter. He didn't care that she was the worst cook in the world. She was here and she was his; he didn't need food.

After dinner they sat side by side in front of their tent, talking quietly of the day's events, listening to the sounds of children's voices, a mother's lullaby, the blare of music from a portable radio, the barking of a camp dog.

They talked of the day's events, of the men he trained, of the women who were becoming her friends. She asked him questions about the coming war.

"War is not the concern of women," he said.

That made her angry, but she didn't give up. She liked to talk about affairs of state, things that he considered a man's domain. She asked about Azrou Jadida and the coming battle. She even made suggestions on how best to defend his country.

He was outraged; he was intrigued. He'd never known a woman like her.

She was a constant delight, a constant surprise, stubborn, enchanting, determined. She had a will of her own that at times had him muttering ancient Bedouin curses.

There were times when she made love with the shy reticence of a virginal bride. And other times when she shocked him with her passion.

One evening when he came in later than usual from training Youssef's men she was behind the curtain where they kept the tin tub. He started to draw it back, but she said, "No, don't!"

He stepped back a pace, surprised.

"Sit down," she said. "I'll be out in a minute."

He stretched out on some of the pillows, wondering what in the world had gotten into her.

Fifteen minutes went by. Twenty. Dammit all, he was hungry. What in the hell was going on? He heard music coming from behind the curtain. A hand appeared. Then a bare foot. And Josie.

A veil covered her face, revealing only her eyes. Her hair fell in soft waves down her back. She wore gold loop

earrings, bracelets on her wrists and bangles around he
ankles.

Her breasts were barely covered with a swath of se
quined chiffon. She wore a thin strip of bikini pantie
under a skirt of a material so sheer he could see every
curve of her pale, spectacular legs.

Her stomach was bare.

Eyes lowered she began to dance to the music of the
radio. Arabic music. Arms raised above her head she
moved slowly toward him, her body swaying to the mu
sic. When she raised her head he saw that her eyes, the
only part of her face that showed above the veil, were
made up with kohl. She looked different, mysterious,
exotic.

For a moment he couldn't get his breath. He felt his
temperature rise. Excitement flared his nostrils.

Her hips moved to the music as she swayed toward
him, then away. The music quickened and so did her
movements. Her hips rotated, slowly, seductively. She
bent her head and swirled her hair over her breasts, her
shoulders and her back. She came toward him and he
felt the soft curtain of her hair against his face. He
reached out for her, but before he could catch her she
had retreated.

The rhythm of the music increased. So did the rhythm
of her hips. His mouth went dry; his body hardened.
He'd never been so excited.

Her body moved so sensuously it was all he could do
not to throw her down on the sand and mount her. The
beat of the music filled his ears. She fell to her knees,
back arched, arms raised, her sweat-slick body still undulating to the frantic rhythm.

She came toward him on her knees, her body swaying, breasts moving. The music reached a crescendo and she fell forward into his arms, gasping for breath.

"My God!" he whispered. "My God!"

He gripped her shoulders and brought her up to him. He kissed her mouth, and when he felt her almost naked breasts pushing against his chest, he eased her down onto the pillows. He ripped off the skirt and the small strip of panties.

Panting with the effort to breathe, she said, "Did you like it? Did you . . ."

He yanked his robe over his head. "I'll show you how much I like it," he said between clenched teeth. "I'll show you what you do to me."

He grasped her sweat-slick hips and before she could say anything, he thrust hard into her.

Half mad with the passion she had roused, he tore off the swatch of material that covered her breasts, and when they were bare he took a nipple between his teeth to bite and suck and lap with his tongue.

She lifted her body to his, giving, receiving. And clutched at his shoulders to bring him closer.

He thrust hard against her. Again and again. Suddenly it was as if a million light bulbs exploded inside his head. He moved like a man possessed, grinding his body to hers, lost in her.

She cupped his face between her hands. She kissed him and took his cry. She said, "Darling. Darling."

He collapsed over her and held her as if he would never let her go. She was everything he had ever wanted in a woman. Everything he had ever dreamed of: lover, companion, friend. She took him to heights of passion he had never imagined existed.

He held her close and his heart beat like the heart o
a captured falcon. How can I let her go? he thought
Dear God, how can I ever let her go?

It was on the same night that the man Abdeslem cam
calling from outside their tent.

"It is my wife," Abdeslem said when Kumar threw
robe on and went to open the flap. "She has delivere
three children without any trouble, but she is having suc
difficulty birthing our fourth that I fear for her life."

"Is there no midwife?"

"Elzaker," Abdeslem said wringing his hands. "Bu
she is away, visiting a sister who is ill. Your woman ha
helped you and others in the camp. I beg you to let he
help my wife."

"Of course, I'll help her," Josie said, and with Ab
deslem leading the way, she and Kumar hurried to th
other tent.

The two men waited outside while she examined th
woman. The baby had crowned, but the head was too
large. She spoke reassuringly to the expectant mother
"I'll help you," she said. "Don't be afraid. But yo
mustn't push. You must wait until I tell you to push."

She held the woman's hand and showed her how to
pant. She asked for boiling water, a knife, scissors,
needle and thread.

"You'll have to help me," she said to Kumar. "Bring
an extra lantern, I'll need all the light I can get."

"What are you going to do?" he asked nervously.
And in English, "Is she going to die?"

Josie shook her head. "Not if I can help it."

Kumar brought the extra lantern. A woman the husband had summoned brought the other things Josie had
asked for.

She told Kumar to hold one of the lanterns higher. To the husband, she said, "I'm going to have to make an incision. I want you to hold your wife's hands."

He swallowed hard. "It is not proper for Sheikh Kumar or me to be here," he said.

Josie looked up from his wife and glared at him. As calmly as she could, she said, "Your wife needs you. Without our help she won't be able to have this baby. You must do as I say for her sake."

She picked up the knife. "Hold her," she said, and made the needed episiotomy.

"Push now," she told the woman. "It's going to be all right, but now you must push."

The woman's face twisted in agony.

"Push!" Josie said again.

The baby came in a rush, and when she held him up and gently slapped him, he howled his "I-wanna-go-back-where-I-came-from" howl.

"It's a boy," she told the mother and father. She laid him down on the clean sheet the other woman had ready, and turned to attend the mother.

Kumar watched her. He'd been sure the woman was going to die, and shocked to find that having a baby could be so painful. But Josie hadn't been afraid, she'd been strong and sure, and she'd surprised him with her skill.

When at last she eased the mother back against the pillows, she took the baby, bathed and wrapped it in a clean white cloth. She held it for a moment then, and kissed its tiny fingers. She looked down at the red face and brushed her fingers across its cheek.

Kumar felt his insides grow weak. In the lantern light her face was more beautiful than it had ever been, her expression so tender he wanted to reach out and touch her.

A little while ago she had been a wanton, now she was a saint, an earth mother bringing a new life into the world.

Who was she? How could he live the rest of his life without her?

At last she handed the baby, almost reluctantly it seemed to him, to the mother.

"You're going to be all right now," she said. "But if you need anything or if you want me, send your husband and I will come."

"Shukran," the new mother whispered. *"Shukran."*

Abdeslem embraced Kumar and kissed him on both cheeks before he, too, said *"Shukran,"* and shook hands with Josie.

They were silent for a while on their way back to their tent, but at last Kumar said, "What you did tonight was remarkable. I've never seen anything like that before. I've never seen a baby born. It's...it's like..." He shook his head, unable to find the words.

"A small miracle," Josie said.

"Yes." He hesitated. "But is it always that painful?"

"Not always."

"How do women stand it? Why do they?"

"Did you see the mother's face when I gave her her baby?"

He nodded.

"Then you know why."

When they were once again in their bed, he put his arms around her, but he made no attempt to make love. Two things had happened tonight that had somehow changed him. He had to think about them.

Chapter 16

They were asleep when the first shots were fired.

"What is it?" Josie sat up, clutching the sheet to her.

"Get down!" Kumar pulled her off the bed and shoved her onto the rug. Gunfire cracked, men screamed. Just outside their tent came the pounding of horses' hooves and warlike cries of "Kill! Kill!"

Kumar pulled a robe over his head and grabbed his gun and bandolier. What in the hell was happening? Who was attacking? My God! Where had they come from?

He ran out of the tent. The attackers, black robes flying out behind them like demons from hell, rode headlong at the camp. They fired as they came and their scimitars flashed in the glow of dying campfires.

A rider bore down on him. In the glow of firelight he saw it was one of the men he had seen in Ben Fatah's tent. He fired; the man clutched his chest and fell. These were Ben Fatah's men! They had come, as Youssef had said, to strike in the dark of the night.

A woman screamed. Kumar whirled around and saw Zaida running toward the pond. A horseman galloped after her, raised his gun and fired. Zaida ran a few more steps, staggered as if drunk, and fell facedown in the sand. The horseman wheeled, and when he did Kumar shot him.

Then he was in the fray, Saoud beside him, firing at the riders who rode toward him. All around were the cries and shouts of the battling men, the screams of women, the terrified shrieks of children.

Other riders rode in with blazing torches held high above their heads, devils of the night, come to kill and plunder and burn.

Kumar ran forward, gun blazing. A scimitar flashed out, but before the rider could bring down the blade he screamed and fell. Kumar turned. Saoud blew on the end of his gun, grinned and kept firing.

A horseman with a torch raced toward Kumar's tent. He pulled his arm back to throw and Kumar shot him—just as Josie ran from the tent.

"Get back!" he shouted.

But she stood frozen, looking about her in horror, barefoot, her hair streaming down her back. She saw the fallen men. And Zaida, facedown in the sand. Before Kumar could stop her, Josie turned and ran toward the fallen woman.

"No!" he shouted. "Come back!" He started after her, caught a sleeve of her robe, grabbed her hand.

"It's Zaida," she cried, trying to get away from him. "She's hurt!"

"Josie, no..." A shot zinged past his ear. He whirled and saw Ben Fatah bearing down on him. He raised his gun to fire but the man and horse were too close, so close he could see the maniacal gleam in Ben Fatah's eyes, the terrified rolled-up whites of the horse's eyes, and could smell the horse's sweat.

He let go of Josie's hand and pushed her out of the way. The horse veered. Ben Fatah bent low in his saddle and with a triumphant cry swept Josie up in front of him.

She screamed and struggled to break free, but he held her tight, jerked hard on the reins and the horse turned and galloped toward the desert.

Ben Fatah! Oh my God! Ben Fatah had taken Josie!

It took Kumar a moment to react. Another rider bore down on him. He reached up and yanked the man down off the saddle and threw himself onto the horse's back. With a cry he drove the animal through the thick of the battle, through screaming bullets and flashing scimitars, whipping it on toward the edge of the camp.

A terrible madness screamed through his brain. Josie! Ben Fatah had taken Josie!

It happened so fast she hadn't had time to think. She'd rushed from her tent into a scene from hell: blazing torches, men shouting, women screaming. Zaida facedown in the sand. She saw the horseman bearing down on Kumar. His eyes were blazing with hellish fury, his gun was raised. But he didn't fire. He'd jerked the reins and the horse came at her.

Kumar! Had she screamed his name?

She fought her captor, trying to turn so that she could strike out. She raked his face with her nails and he hit her on the side of the head. For a moment everything went black. She struggled for breath and to clear her head. Who was he? Dear God, where was he taking her?

"Let me go!" She struggled against the arm that tightened like a band of steel around her waist. Sand from the horse's flying hooves stung her face.

"Kumar's woman!" her captor shouted. "I have taken Kumar Ben Ari's woman!" He laughed, but suddenly the laughter died. He looked behind him and with a curse he reached for his gun.

She heard the pounding of horses' hooves. A horse and rider pulled alongside.

"Kumar!" she cried. "Kumar!"

Ben Fatah leveled his gun. Josie shouted a warning and struck his wrist. The gun flew out of his hand.

Kumar reached out and grabbed the reins of the other horse and yanked with every bit of his strength. The animal jerked and reared and when it did Josie slipped from Ben Fatah's grasp and fell to the sand. Kumar hung on. Ben Fatah's horse whinnied in terror and came to a sudden stop.

Ben Fatah jumped off, reaching for the jeweled dagger as he slid to the sand. Before he could pull it out of the scabbard, Kumar was on him, grappling, fists flying. Ben Fatah staggered back and they fell together to the sand.

Josie got up from where she'd fallen and ran toward them. The moon had gone behind a cloud and in the desert darkness it was almost impossible to see which man was which. Then the moon came out from behind the clouds and Josie saw Kumar pinned under the other man. She heard their grunts and muttered curses. She saw the other man draw a dagger from his belt.

She ran forward, breath tight in her throat, panting with effort, bare feet sinking in the sand. The man who had captured her raised his arm. She saw the gleam of a knife and without thinking scooped up a handful of sand and flung it in his face.

He cried out and tried to scrub the sand away. Kumar hit him and he fell back. The two of them scrambled on the sand for the fallen knife. Ben Fatah reached it first, grasped it and slashed out. Kumar feinted to one side and grabbed his arm.

The moon disappeared behind the clouds again, but still the two men fought on, cursing, panting with effort. As Josie watched in horror the knife was raised. It slashed down and a terrible cry rent the air.

She staggered forward, calling, "Kumar! Kumar!"

He rolled away from the other man. "It's ... it's all right." He got to his feet and she ran to him.

"Is he dead?"

"Yes." He smothered her face against his shoulder. "Yes."

He cupped her face between his hands. "Are you all right?"

"Now." She clung to him. "Now I am."

He held her close. I've killed a man, he thought. And I would do it again. I would do anything I had to to protect her.

He tightened his arms around her and held her as if he would never let her go.

"I love you," he said against the tangle of her hair. "Dear God, Josie. I didn't know. I didn't know how much."

He kissed her closed eyelids, her nose, her cheeks, and his eyes misted with all that he was feeling. He had almost lost her and the thought of that filled him with a fear unlike anything he had ever known.

Now that Ben Fatah was dead there was little fear that his men would attack again. But the camp was in shambles. Some of the tents had been burned, men had been killed, more had been wounded. Zaida was dead.

The next few days passed in a blur of activity. A tent was set up for the wounded. Pots of water were put to boil. White robes were torn into strips for bandages. There was no time for Josie to think of what had happened, no time to remember her fear or the words of love Kumar had spoken. Men and women were injured, she had to take care of them.

A modern hospital, *any* hospital, would have been appalled at the conditions under which she worked. God knows she would have been called before a board of inquiry for doing the work only a doctor should do.

But there was no one else if lives were to be saved. She stitched sword wounds, dug out bullets and sewed a half-severed ear back on.

She comforted the women whose husbands had been injured and held the hands of a dying man. She sat beside little Rafi, whose shoulder had been shattered by a bullet, and told him stories about planes and trains and cars, and promised that when she took him back to the city so that his shoulder could be properly repaired she would make sure he had a ride in Kumar's private plane.

In the back of her mind, as Josie worked with what little she had, she thought about what she could do at the hospital once she returned to Bir Chagga. The operating room there should be expanded. More trained professionals were needed. She'd already made a vast improvement, but there was still so much to be done. In addition there were the clinics she wanted to set up all around the country, so that rural people could have the same care as those in the city.

So much to do.

If she stayed.

Little by little as she took care of them, these people became her people and she knew that when it came time to leave the Bedouin camp she would not want to go.

Because of the demands on her time, she'd had little opportunity to think about the new phase in her relationship with Kumar. There was a part of her that was grateful she didn't have to. Not yet. She wasn't ready to deal with it yet.

She was glad that at night when she returned to their tent all she could think about was getting a few hours of sleep. She fell into bed so exhausted she could do little more than whisper "'Night," before she fell asleep in his arms.

But at odd times during the day, when she was taking care of a patient or telling a story to Rafi, she would suddenly think, Kumar loves me. He told me he loves me. She would relive again that terrifying ride across the desert and remember the fear she had known when the two men struggled on the sand.

And later the words, Kumar's words: "I love you."

They hadn't talked about it. He was as busy preparing the men for battle as she was tending the wounded. But he came to the makeshift hospital whenever he could, to see if he could help.

"Are you all right?" he asked again and again. "You're worn out. You need to rest."

A week passed before Josie's patients were well enough for their wives and the other women to see to some of their care. Late one afternoon, when she knew that her patients were out of danger and that they would be taken care of, she left the tent and walked out toward the rise of dunes. She needed to sleep, but even more than sleep she needed to be alone for a little while.

It was that time just before sunset when she climbed to the rise of a dune and looked out over the desert. It was a quiet, almost holy time of day. The sky caught fire in a blaze of breathtaking colors—blue mingled with flamingo orange, and a red so brilliant it hurt Josie's eyes. As she watched, the darker blue changed to a softer blue tinged with green and stripes of pink, and the sands of the desert turned to gold.

Below lay the city of black tents and the people who were Kumar's people. Kumar, her desert sheikh. A man different from any other man.

As she watched, she saw him striding toward her through the sand. His dark robe billowed out behind him and his midnight black hair was ruffled by the breeze that always came this time of day.

"I saw you from below," he said when he reached her. "Why did you not come to the tent?"

"I needed a walk." She reached for his hand and faced the setting sun. "I love this time of day, Kumar. The heat lessens, a soft wind comes off the desert and everything is so quiet, so peaceful."

He put his arms around her waist and she leaned back against him. "There's no sunset quite like the sunset on the desert, is there?" she said.

"No, *laeela.*" He kissed the top of her head and held her for a long time without speaking. But finally, because he knew she had to be told, he said, "I've had word from my father. Azrou Jadida has invaded our borders. They're marching toward the city."

"You're going to leave."

He nodded. "I've sent word to the other desert tribes. As soon as they come we'll leave for Bir Chagga."

She turned so that she could see his face. "Am I to go with you?"

"No, Josie. You'll wait here in the camp with the other women until I return." He touched her hair. The last rays of the setting sun had turned it the color of fire. He stroked it and gently kissed her. "Do not look so," he said. "I will go, but I will return."

"You're going into battle." She clutched the front of his robe and fought for control. "I know you have to go, Kumar, but I don't want you to. The thought of you being in danger..." She leaned her head against his chest so he wouldn't see the fear in her eyes.

"When the war is over I'll come back for you. We have many things to talk about, yes? And many decisions to make."

He had not spoken of the words he had uttered the night of her abduction, but now he must speak of them. He must speak to her of many things.

"I thought I had lost you the night the camp was attacked," he said. "The night Ben Fatah carried you away. I've never known such terror, Josie, for if I had lost you..." He stopped, unable for a moment to go on. "I knew then what I had known all along but had not been willing to face. I knew that I loved you, that I would kill for you." He put his arms around her and held her close. "I would die for you, Josie. I can't live my life without you."

He cupped her chin so that she would look at him. "I know we're very different. I know there will be problems, things about my country that you'll never understand. But the thought of losing you..." He shook his head. "I won't lose you," he said in a voice shaking with emotion. "I love you. I can't let you go."

"Kumar..." All kinds of conflicting emotions, like the glass of a kaleidoscope, twirled round and round, skittered through her mind. We're too different... Impossible... I couldn't live in his world. Would he live in mine? But if I love him... Dear God, of course I love him. If I do, then how can I leave him? And for what? Another job in another country? Another man. Oh, no! No, there could never be anyone but Kumar for me.

"Tell me," he said. "Tell me you love me."

"I love you," she said. "Of course I do."

"Then marry me, Josie. Stay with me. Live with me."

"Darling..." She took a breath to steady herself. "I don't know," she whispered. "There are so many things separating us. Different ideas. Different worlds." Her voice gentled. "I'd have to give up my world to live in yours, Kumar. I'm not sure I can do that."

She leaned her head against his chest, holding him as he held her. "This time with you in the desert has been..." She searched for the words to tell him what this had meant to her and about the joy that being with him had brought. But all she could say was, "This has been the happiest time of my life, but I'm afraid... I'm so afraid it won't last. Because we're different. Because—"

"Because of the way you feel about Middle Eastern men. Arabs like me." His eyes narrowed and his mouth tightened with anger. "Because you still class all of us in with Jenny's ex-husband and Ben Fatah."

"Oh, no, Kumar, no. Not since I first came to your country, not since I met men like Saoud and Youssef and so many others." She kissed him. "And you, Kumar," she whispered against his lips. "And you." She leaned close into him and with her face against his shoulder said, "I'm ashamed of my prejudice. I ask your forgiveness for the way I felt, for the things I said before."

He held her away from him. "Do you love me, Josie?"

"Yes, I love you."

"But still you doubt." He tightened his hands on her shoulders. "You don't want to marry me." The words were bitterly spoken. Harsh. "You don't want to live in Abdu Resaba with me."

"I need time," she whispered.

He let her go and turned away from her. In the last rays of the sun, with the wind blowing the dark robe around his ankles and his skin turned the deep, rich color of bronze, he was all desert man. A Bedouin, by birth and by his love for this vast and wonderful land.

She touched his hand. "I'll give you my answer when you return," she said.

He put his arm around her and they stood with their arms around each other as the last rays of the setting sun cast patterns of shade across the rolling dunes and darkness came to the desert. Only then did they go back down the dune to the camp.

The tribes of Amin Elmusa and Abdur Khan began to gather outside the tent city of Youssef Abedi. There were more than three thousand of them and still more came every day to join those already here, dark-skinned men in *djellaba*s and *ghutra*s, a powerful fighting force that, together with Youssef's one thousand warriors, would soon march on Bir Chagga.

There were the thousands of camels the men would ride, plus additional camels to carry the supplies needed for the four-day trip across the desert, as well as their rifles and rounds of ammunition.

It was, Josie thought, as if a giant city had suddenly sprung up in the middle of the desert. Even from their tent she could hear the rumble of the thousands of men's voices and the grumbling snorts of their beasts. At night she could smell the food they prepared and see the glow of their campfires.

They were a strong fighting force and together, with Kumar leading them, they would defend Abdu Resaba against the aggressor.

Josie saw little of Kumar. He spent the last few days before the journey with the men who would ride with him, for they were his brothers—fellow Bedouins who would, if necessary, fight to the death beside him. He sat by their campfires at night and shared their food. They spoke of their homes and of the women they had left behind, as he would leave his woman.

His woman. He prayed to Allah that one day it would be true, that Josie would love him as he loved her. But could she give up the life she knew for the life he was destined to lead here in Abdu Resaba? It would be a life of ease and of luxury, and for as long as his father still ruled he and Josie would be free to travel, to see and to share together some of the beautiful places of the world. If she wanted to continue her work at the hospital he would offer no objection.

But when his father stepped down or died and Kumar became the ruler of Abdu Resaba, things would be different. He would have many duties to attend to, so they would not be able to travel as they had before. And certainly it would not be fitting for the wife of Sheikh Kumar Ben Ari, the titular head of the country, to work in a hospital or any other place.

Would Josie be able to accomodate herself to such a life? Could she give up the world she had known, to become a part of his world?

She can if she loves me, he told himself. If she loves me enough.

* * *

On the night before he was to leave with his men for
Bir Chagga, Kumar returned early to their tent. Josie
had just finished bathing and when he came in he found
her wearing the simple white robe she sometimes slept in.
She was sitting on a low hassock, brushing her hair.

"Mesa al khair," he said when he entered. For indeed it was an evening of goodness whenever he returned to find her waiting for him. He crossed to her,
took the brush from her hand and began to brush her
hair.

"You leave tomorrow," she said.

"Before dawn." He lifted a handful of her hair and let
it drift through his fingers. She leaned back against him
and closed her eyes and when she did he put down the
brush and cupped her breasts.

"We'll make love tonight," he said.

"Oh, yes."

He caressed her, hesitated, and with a note of surprise in his voice asked, "Is it my imagination, or are
your breasts larger than they were?"

The breath caught in her throat. Larger? If they were
did that mean . . . ? They had been in the desert for over
two months, lovers for all of that time. She could have
gotten pregnant that first night. She probably had. Dear
Lord! Fighting for control, not wanting him to know,
she shook her head and said, "No, no, I don't think so."

He picked up the brush again and stroked her hair.
With his other hand he stroked her breast. Stroking,
stroking until her eyes drifted closed again.

There was a closeness in his touch, an intimacy that
only lovers know. She didn't want to move or speak. She
wanted to capture this moment so she could hold it in the

palm of her hand and take out the memory of it when h
was gone from her.

He was leaving to go into the heat of battle, into
danger she could only imagine. She was afraid for him
she didn't want him to go. But he would go and ther
was nothing she could do to keep him here. She coul
only pray to her God and to his Allah to keep him safe

She turned and took the brush from his hand
"Come," she said in a voice that trembled from all sh
was feeling. And taking his hand she led him to thei
bed.

In the golden glow of the lantern light she took off he
robe and stood naked before him. He put his arm
around her and held her close, letting passion wait
content for now with this moment of closeness.

"I love you," he whispered against the fall of her hair

"As I love you." She clung to him, as though by th
force of her love, by holding him in her arms this way
she could keep him safe from the danger that lay ahead

"Don't tremble so," he said, sensing her fear. "
promise that I will come back." He cupped her face be
tween his hands. "Believe," he said. "Believe."

He picked her up and carried her to their bed
Quickly, then, he pulled the robe over his head and ease(
his briefs down over his hips.

He lay down beside her and gathered her into hi
arms.

"My love," he said. He kissed her mouth, gently a
first, then with growing passion. He parted her lips with
his tongue, and when her tongue met his, he sighed with
pleasure.

They kissed like that for a long time, and though thei
naked bodies pressed one to the other, they made them-

selves wait for that ultimate moment when once again their bodies would be joined.

He touched her breasts with gentle hands. Slowly, oh, so slowly, he came closer and closer to the aching peaks. He took each tip in his fingers to squeeze and tease. He ran his fingernails lightly over them and she moaned into his mouth.

"Now I must taste them," he whispered, and bent his head to kiss first one, then the other, and turning Josie onto her side he lay with his head on her arm so that he could lap and kiss and tease at will.

This was his woman, his Josie who threaded her fingers through his hair to hold him close to her breasts. Josie who whispered his name and said, "Oh, yes. That's good. That's so good."

He reached to touch her between her legs, and they parted for him. He fondled her gently, caressing the warm moistness of her, circling around that most tender part, touching until her whispers grew heated and she said, "No more. No more or I will . . ."

"Will what, my love?"

"You know. You know." She tugged at his shoulders. "Come over me," she said. "I want to feel your body on mine. I want to feel you inside me."

He caressed once more that special place, then eased himself over her. "Now, dearest?" he asked.

"Yes." A tremulous sigh. "Oh, yes."

Her legs parted. He felt her softness with that hard and pulsating part of himself, and with a low cry he thrust into her, gasping with the sheer joy of being part of her again. Her warmth took him in, held him, and when he began to move against her, her body rose to meet his.

She loved this. She loved him. When they were together this way there were no yesterdays, no tomorrows, no doubts. There was only the here and now, and the heaven of being in his arms again.

She kissed his mouth. She encircled him with her arms and with her legs.

Their cadence quickened. He thrust harder, deeper. He rubbed his body against hers as if he couldn't get enough of her. He took her lower lip to suckle, then plunged his tongue into her mouth as that other part of him plunged again and again into her body.

This is a madness, he thought in that part of his mind that still functioned, a fever in the blood that only she can cure. He cried her name, "Josie! Josie!" and moved against her with the terrible desperation of all the love he felt for her.

"Ride with me!" he demanded. "Stay with me. Tell me... tell me..."

"Oh, please," she whispered, gone a little mad herself in the wildness of this lovemaking. Then she started over the edge and tried to muffle her cry against his shoulder.

He grasped her chin. "Look at me! Look at me!"

His love-filled eyes were midnight black and flecked with gold in the light of the lantern. "Josie ... Josie."

And when he thrust again she spiraled up and up and her body burst with an ecstasy that was a little like dying.

He covered her mouth with his. He gave her his cry and collapsed over her, his body shaking with all that he was feeling.

When it began to subside they held each other quietly and kissed each other gently. And slept at last in the shelter of each other's arms.

He left before dawn the next day.

Chapter 17

Two weeks went by.

Three.

Four.

There was no news from Bir Chagga. Time and again the women of the camp turned their gazes toward the west, waiting, hoping for a sign of riders.

But there was no sign.

They milked their goats and tended their fields, and spoke in hushed voices—as if a loud sound might shatter the calm acceptance of a fear so terrible they could not speak of it.

When Josie wasn't with them and helping with the chores, she spent her time with little Rafi. His mother was dead, his father was at war. There was only an aging aunt to care for him. His shoulder bandaged, his arm in a sling, he spoke often of how it would be when he went to the big hospital in the city.

"It's not that I will be afraid," he told Josie. "But you will be with me, yes?"

"Of course, I will."

"And when my shoulder is better we'll go in the airplane with Sheikh Ben Ari?"

"Yes, Rafi."

Yes, because she would not let herself believe that Kumar would not come back.

Each night at sunset she climbed to that place on the rise of the dune where they had gone the night before he left. She looked out to the west, her hand shading her eyes, searching for a cloud of dust that meant the men from the camp were returning.

But day after day there was no sign of them.

Often as she stood looking out at the dunes, she rested her hand on her belly, drawing comfort from the child growing there. For she knew now that she was pregnant. And there was gladness in her heart that a part of Kumar was growing inside her.

Every evening as she stood at the top of the dune, she searched her heart for the answer she would give when he returned. I'll know when I see him, she told herself. I'll know if I can give up the life I've always known, to live the life he must live here in Abdu Resaba.

If he were not the son of the ruler, if he were free to travel as he wished, to live in the West for a part of the year, it would be easier. But one day Kumar's father would step down and he would become the head of his country. When that happened, if she married him, she would be bound, as these other women were bound, to stay by his side and to observe all of the customs of his country.

Abdu Resaba was his home. Could it ever be hers?

She loved Kumar with all her heart. But she didn
know if she could ever be the woman he wanted her
be.

Five weeks passed.
Six.
The women in the camp changed their white robes fo
black. They rarely spoke in voices above a whisper. Thei
faces were solemn, their expressions resigned.

Josie refused to wear black. She refused to be re
signed. She played with the children, laughed when the
laughed and spoke to the other women in a norma
voice.

She wouldn't give up hope. Kumar had promised tha
he would return and he would. She had to believe h
would.

And every evening at sunset when she climbed th
dune and stood looking out over the desert, she praye
to her god and to his. She said, "Keep him safe. Brin
him back to me."

One evening when Josie looked toward the west i
seemed to her that she could see a speck of dust on th
horizon. Her heart quickened, for as she watched th
dust became a cloud, then a rider.

With a glad cry she ran down the other side of th
dune, slipping, sliding, stumbling in her haste. Then sh
was running across the sand toward the figure she saw
emerging from the cloud of dust.

"Kumar!" she called out, even though she knew h
was too far away to hear. "Kumar!" Because she knew
it was him. It had to be him.

The white robe billowed out behind the racing camel
The beast came closer, its hooves kicking up the sand a
its rider spurred it on.

Josie ran on, her arms outstretched, because now she could see his face. It was Kumar. He'd come back just as he'd said he would.

He reached her. He called out to her as he pulled on the reins and whacked the animal's knees. When it kneeled, he threw himself out of the saddle and ran to meet her.

She cried his name and then she was in his arms, clinging to him, weeping against his shoulder, touching his face, whispering his name over and over again.

His kissed her and his mouth was hungry on hers. "This is the moment I've dreamed of," he said, when he held her away from him.

"Are you all right?" She clutched his shoulders as if to assure herself he was really here. "Is it over?"

"It's over. Sharif Kadiri is dead. Azrou Jadida surrendered two weeks ago." His expression grew solemn, his eyes were sad. "We lost a lot of good men, Josie. But yes, it's over."

"Saoud?" she asked anxiously. "Youssef?"

"They're a half day's ride behind me. I couldn't wait, I had to get to you as soon as I could." He touched her face. "Has it been bad for you?" he asked. "Are you all right."

She thought, then, that she should tell him about the child she was carrying. His child. But she hesitated. What would he say? Would he be happy that together they had created a new life?

"Josie?" He looked concerned. "Is anything wrong? Are you all right?"

She took his hand and laid it on her stomach. With a smile she said, "I'm as all right as a woman who's pregnant can be."

His face went still. "Are you sure?"

"I'm a nurse, Kumar. A nurse who was so in love she forgot all about birth control. Of course I'm sure."

He closed his hands on her shoulders. "You won't leave me," he said in a voice that shook with all he was feeling.

"Of course I won't leave you."

"You'll marry me."

"Just as soon as I can."

With a glad cry he pulled her back into his arms. Josie, his life, his love. Soon she would be his wife, the mother of his child.

He cupped her face between his hands and asked, "What of the differences you were so concerned about?"

"We'll work them out. If we love each other..."

"We love," he said.

He kissed her and she knew that it was true. They loved. And that, after all, was all that mattered.

*   *   *   *   *

Fifty red-blooded, white-hot, true-blue hunks
from every State in the Union!

Look for MEN MADE IN AMERICA! Written by some of
our most popular authors, these stories feature fifty of the
strongest, sexiest men, each from a different state in the
union!

Two titles available every month at your favorite retail
outlet.

In July, look for:

ROCKY ROAD by Anne Stuart (Maine)
THE LOVE THING by Dixie Browning (Maryland)

In August, look for:

PROS AND CONS by Bethany Campbell (Massachusetts)
TO TAME A WOLF by Anne McAllister (Michigan)

You won't be able to resist MEN MADE IN AMERICA!

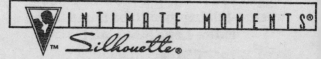

Return to Southern Alberta's rustic ranch land as Judith Duncan's Wide Open Spaces miniseries continues in July with THAT SAME OLD FEELING, IM#577.

Chase McCall had come home a new man. Yet painful memories—and an old but familiar lover—awaited his return. Devon Manyfeathers had refused him once, but one look into her soulful brown eyes had Chance focusing on forever.

And there will be more McCalls to meet in future months, as they learn love's lessons in the wide open spaces of Western Canada.

SILHOUETTE® Desire®

They're sexy, they're determined, they're trouble with a capital *T!*

Meet six of the steamiest, most stubborn heroes you'd ever want to know, and learn *everything* about them....

August's *Man of the Month,* Quinn Donovan, in **FUSION** by Cait London

Mr. Bad Timing, Dan Kingman, in **DREAMS AND SCHEMES** by Merline Lovelace

Mr. Marriage-phobic, Connor Devlin, in **WHAT ARE FRIENDS FOR?** by Naomi Horton

Mr. Sensible, Lucas McCall, in **HOT PROPERTY** by Rita Rainville

Mr. Know-it-all, Thomas Kane, in **NIGHTFIRE** by Barbara McCauley

Mr. Macho, Jake Powers, in **LOVE POWER** by Susan Carroll

Look for them on the covers so you can see just how handsome and irresistible they are!

Coming in August only from Silhouette Desire!   CENTER

Don't miss the newest miniseries from
Silhouette Intimate Moments

Southern
Knights

by Marilyn Pappano

A police detective. An FBI agent. A government
prosecutor. Three men for whom friendship and
the law mean everything. Three men for whom
true love has remained elusive—until now. Join
award-winning author Marilyn Pappano as she
brings her **Southern Knights** series to you, starting
in August 1994 with MICHAEL'S GIFT, IM #583.

The visions were back. And detective
Michael Bennett knew well the danger they
prophesied. Yet he couldn't refuse to help
beautiful fugitive Valery Navarre, not after her
image had been branded on his mind—and
his heart.

Then look for Remy's story in December, as
Southern Knights continues, only in...